A STRANGER LEAVES

Adam Lee Parry

A STRANGER LEAVES

Vanguard Press

A CIP catalogue record for this title is
available from the British Library.

ISBN 978 1 784658 38 0

*Vanguard Press is an imprint of
Pegasus Elliot MacKenzie Publishers Ltd.*
www.pegasuspublishers.com

First Published in 2020

**Vanguard Press
Sheraton House Castle Park
Cambridge England**

Printed & Bound in Great Britain

Dedication

I would like to dedicate this book to my father, Ron Parry, who died in 2018.

Part 1

Chapter One

It was precisely nine p.m. and after his bath the music on the computer came to an end. He wondered if he should clean his teeth again, but decided not to. Cleaning them earlier had been a Herculean task that had woken the child next door and set her off wailing maniacally.

He dressed in his finery: clean jeans with no trendy holes, a blank black T-shirt tucked in tight, finally his blue buttoned shirt which highlighted the attempt at a potbelly that he had garnered of late. He took his anti-psychotics and anti-epileptics.

I'm ready, he told himself as he booted up, his new coat half on as he stepped out and locked the door behind him.

He chased after his shadow down the hill hoping he would reach the bus stop in time. He groaned when he saw that no one else was waiting, and stoically resigned himself to a long sojourn. He tried to distract himself with stars and the pine trees at the amber lit turn in the road. *I wish I'd brought my camera. Stop wishing!* he reprimanded himself. Yet he had sneezed earlier so he allowed himself this one. He forced himself to wait.

After a cigarette the bus came with a weary slowness toward the stop.

The bright lights in the bus made him feel covered in stains, made him remember a dream which he forgot, as he took a seat. Apart from a couple of women in the seat in front of him and the driver, the bus was empty. The air smelled stale and he anxiously fidgeted his feet on the carpet of discarded tickets.

Surprisingly the eight miles into town seemed to pass in no time. He bought a burger and ate it walking along the pavement — eyes fastened on the many bare legs going this way and that. He considered that it was rude to stare but decided, seeing as he hadn't been further than the chemist in about a year, he was sure the good Lord didn't mind that much.

Near the Castlegate he went down to a bar called Characters and was lured in by a builder's bottom. A builder's bottom though both slim and shapely, the builder's bottom owner with her cascade of hair like a black waterfall topping her off.

She was putting on an Adele Adkins song on the jukebox when he went in.

'Oh, no, not that, it always makes me cry,' he said to her. She sort of smiled. After a while he sat near the corner table where she sat with an empty bottle of wine and a licked clean glass in front of her. After a brief, cack-handed attempt at a conversation with her, dejectedly he sunk his pint and left.

Outside the Moorings the crowd of smokers halted his way forward. He looked through the window of the pub at the teeming mob within. As he went in a bouncer told him it was three quid entry — he forked out thankfully. Only just in the door, he saw an acquaintance. Dave. Dave Somebody. Poet-guy. Cyber Punk was playing along with a tad of Neo-Goth. There were people everywhere. It took a while to get a drink and when he got to his seat, he turned for no reason, and saw the girl from Characters.

'You follow me?'

She laughed. 'Could you get me a double vodka and lemonade?' She thrust a fiver at him. He went back to the bar, reluctantly gave the girl her change — she stared off into the distance as if he had suddenly disappeared.

For a while she seemed to disappear and he got talking to a black-lipped lesbian wearing a tie and to her freckled partner sitting on her knee. A guy called Two showed them the studs pierced into his back, two lines of them parallel with his spine like someone had hammered carpet tacks into him. The girl from Characters had left her vodka and lemonade untended, so he purloined it and necked it in a oner.

The lesbians left and Dave Somebody had long gone. Two had fallen asleep. He needed a smoke. Outside the dark-haired girl stood. She asked: 'Can you take me to your place?'

Before she changed her mind, he frogmarched her up to the taxi rank. Inside, on the way home, she lay with her head on his lap, while he gently fingered her and told the dark glints of her eyes, 'I want to fuck your eyes.'

Back home they fumbled in drunken embraces. He kissed as if he had forgotten the taste of kisses. His kisses and small nips of teeth bites lingered, lowering by increments down her abdomen. He licked, and lured moans from her mouth. She came so gently, so gently her nails bit into his hands. Not too soon after that she fell asleep.

He paced, he pondered. He wanted to sketch her pale form half-hidden beneath the duvet cast about her.

He paced, went back to see if she was still asleep. She was.

He took some extra anti-psychotics, an anti-epileptic or two, and two and a half anti-depressants. Still he couldn't sleep and went back to pacing, just staring at her and listening to her gentle snores. At some point before dawn he must've fallen asleep.

The next two days he spent going down to the newsagents for Helen's wine and going down on her. To his surprise she told him she was twenty-one going on twenty-two. He'd surmised that she could be no older than seventeen. She was a drop out from Psychology School, but was now studying alcohol in all its forms. Despite dropping out of University she was soon psychoanalysing Ash. He caught her reading his diary

14

and she quickly interrogated out of him that he had a schizophrenic disorder and was one of the best book thieves in that particular part of Scotland.

'How many people have you slept with?' Helen asked.

'I don't know. I don't keep count. You are the first person I have had sex with since the middle of the last decade.'

She didn't seem to be impressed with this.

'What about you?'

'I've had four or five boyfriends. I lived with a couple of them, but there's an old guy on the top floor of our tenement who gives me a £100 to pose for him, but that's not exactly sex. Can I use your telephone?'

She did for about an hour or two. By then it was about five p.m. She'd been on the phone to her dad. Ash thought she was going to cry — but he realised she wasn't the kind of person who breaks down in tears; as if she knew by experience that it never brought what she needed.

Tentatively he asked, 'Did he hit you?'

'No. He had an affair and left me and mum — she started drinking too much. She wasn't an alkie like me, but she got really depressed.'

'I don't know him, but you know,' Ash said, 'he's probably regretting everything he said to you. When my dad was in hospital last year he said he wished he'd never spent his whole life being angry. I'm old enough to be your father and I'm sure if your dad was anything like him it would break his heart seeing you like this.'

'You think so?' she said and for the first time since she'd spoken to him these last three days there seemed to be hope in her voice.

The taxi she'd asked him to call for her arrived. He watched her from the hallway, fragile-framed by the door. She did not look back or see him wave.

A few days later Alison's cocaine-calm voice answered when Ash rang needing someone to talk to.

'The Moorings,' she purred. 'That's one of the most haunted pubs up here.'

'Yeah?'

'It used to be a coaching house way back.'

'Where did you hear about that?'

'In one of my mum's books about local history. Barrels and tables would slide across the dance floor back in the nineties. Some bar staff said they heard voices coming up from the cellar through the trapdoor behind the bar. Oh yeah, the beer taps would stop working, or the lights and the jukebox, and when the engineers came in there was nothing wrong with them, then a few days later they'd all go off again one by one until the engineers got sick of them calling.'

Ash laughed. 'Maybe we should do ghost tours of all the haunted pubs in town and charge the tourists a packet. I'm sure they do stuff like that in Edinburgh.'

They chatted a while longer but after hanging up he could not stop thinking about the haunted Moorings.

At times over the next two weeks, Ash found himself haunting the Moorings looking for Helen. It wasn't until the third Saturday after they first met, and in a somewhat less rowdy bar, that Helen walked in. She looked smart. He was getting a Budvar and she came over to the bar and he told her she was looking good.

'I had an interview for a job at Snafu.'

'Did you get it?'

'They said they'd phone.'

They went and sat at an empty table. He asked a lot of questions out of nervousness but he seemed to be talking to a brick wall. Within ten minutes she had fallen asleep on his chest.

The bar manager and the bouncer were taking a particular interest in them. Ash squirmed. He tried to wake her up. Eventually the bouncer helped Ash struggle her out of the bar into the crisp, cold night of the smoker's pavement. How he got her to the taxi rank amazed him. Helen remained in a vaguely conscious state as the line ahead of them dwindled. Ash's anxiety levels grew as only a few couples ahead of them remained, because Helen was snoring on her feet. At last theirs arrived and, with the help of one of the taxi marshals in an iridescent yellow jacket, he got her in the taxi. She almost lay down on the back seat. It seemed pointless trying to put a seatbelt on her. She swayed and shifted with each turn and twist round bends the taxi driver made so he held her tight to him so she wouldn't hurt herself.

'There's just one more corner,' he reassured her. 'Then it's all a long straight stretch home.'

He sat her at the kitchen table and made her some noodles. She helped herself to a container of cherry tomatoes and they shared a bar of chocolate. Ash took her through to the sofa and she remained there alone until the next afternoon.

She came through to Ash's bedroom.

'Will you go down on me?'

He laughed. 'My nose is still recovering from the abrasions of our last sessions.' But he didn't want to nay say her — he enjoyed imaging tendrils of flame emanating from the tip of his tongue, raging the flames into her, opening all the pores of her body as if he were some sexual magician. Yes, he enjoyed it — it seemed to Ash that he wore a clear plastic space helmet that domed up from his head encasing her belly and buttocks, flowing back round to his agitated tongue and lips.

That night and the next day the snow came. Ash presumed she would want to go home, but she'd ripped the skirt she'd been wearing, only had opened-toed silver shoes and a T-shirt that wouldn't keep the chill out even in Ibiza in July. Yet she insisted they go to the RBS so she could pay her share of the taxi fare and the wine he'd bought before.

He dressed her in his favourite black jeans. They wouldn't button up for him anymore but fitted her like a condom on a penis. He threw on her a baggy black and white sweater and gave her a pair of oversized sneakers. He looked out at the snow teeming down, put over his pyjama bottoms a pair of trousers, fitted a second set of socks, two thick fleeces, and his Christmas coat.

When they finally got to the bank the fucking thing was closed. Oh well, he thought, another trip to the offie with my debit card.

But the snow was beautiful, made more so by the fairness of his village and Helen beside him. He said hello, as he usually did, to people passing,

'Do you know them?' Helen wondered.

'Not all of them, it's just the way it is here.' He remembered how seemingly friendless the city had been back before he came to the village up the valley from the River Dee.

He loaded up with cash in his own thankfully open bank and, despite knowing they would have to walk all the way up the hill, they encumbered themselves with three bags of groceries and a rather bogging hot dog. Being twenty-one going on twenty-two ascending the hill wasn't so bad for her, but Ash puffed, panted, groaned, took more than the occasional rest until they were back thrusting themselves through the door and dumping the bags at their feet, until they caught their breaths, like they were exhibitions in a surrealist art show.

By the time Ash got round to putting all the messages away, Helen had drunk the bottle of rosé and was making good speed on the paltry white. She asked him if she could use the phone again. Of course, he said, but then got in a bit of a mood when she asked him to give her some privacy while she talked. He went and lay on the bed, not really eavesdropping but most of what she said he could clearly hear through the wall.

First, she called the STD clinic and found out that she had Chlamydia. Next, and for about an hour, she spoke to her dad, a dentist. He seemed to have disowned her, or she him, when she dropped out of uni. Each strain and sound of her voice seemed to yearn for some forgiveness from him until she finally gave up as if knowing she would never hear the words, 'I love you, I'm sorry.'

Then Ash heard a thud. He rushed through.

'Helen! Helen!' he called. She'd fallen from the computer chair and lay curled up the floor in a vast soaking stain of wine. Or urine? He should try and lift her up, shouldn't he? He thought about it. She wasn't that big, but he was middle-aged, smoked too much, and hadn't picked up anything heavier than a book for a long time.

He escaped back in the bedroom worrying about it. For an hour or so. I'm being selfish, he derided himself and finally went back through to her. Psyching himself up like an Olympic weightlifter he got his arms under her as if he were not just carrying Helen, but all the heavy weight of her twenty-one going on twenty-two years of life. He raised her and carried her to the sofa. Ash switched off the light leaving the room pitch black and presumed she would sleep and he could too. Of course he couldn't. He called up Alison.

'High?' he said nervously.

'Certainly am. Sorry I didn't call you back. My daughter came up just as you called.'

'She's here,' he blurted. 'Not your daughter. Helen. Helen's here. She just passed out. I don't know what to do.'

'Is she breathing?'

Ash looked over.

'Yes, I think so. I don't want to call an ambulance. What do you think?'

'Get a grip, she's probably just pissed.'

'Wish I was.' He heard Helen snore, not as gently as before, as if she had reached a place in her dreams, way up high where the air was thin.

He apologized for bothering Alison as it was three a.m. and they dragged the conversation out a bit before he he hung up.

Helen still slept.

Ash called his oldest, dearest friend, Martha, who lived in a wee village outside Edinburgh. He had first met her in 1990. Christ! Twenty-two years ago. She had the same birthday as his mum. They'd met in a playwriting workshop. Then a year or so later he developed his schizophrenia. She wrote to him in the asylum.

He'd seen a news item about a gardener reproducing an immense field into a copy of Vincent van Gogh's *Sunflowers*. Before he'd even mentioned it to her, like synchronicity, or a coincidence, or perhaps just life, she sent him a postcard with an aerial photograph on the front of it.

When he got out of the asylum, she took him to the sunflower field and Ash wondered if he hadn't been on so much medication could he, too, have made something as beautiful as this.

'Hi, Martha.'

'Ash,' she said croakily.

'So you've still got your flu.'

'Afraid so.'

'I met her again!'

'Who?'

'Helen.' Duh. 'She's here and snoring.'

'So you've got a woman in your bed so you've decided to call me.'

'I made her sleep on the couch.'

Martha laughed lightly and coughed.

'Anyway, I was wondering if I can come down and see you?'

A pause. 'Why not? I'm free until the ninth then some friends from Chester are staying.'

'Hey. I was on your blog and I saw you've a new book out.'

'Haven't I sent you a copy?' she asked.

'No, but I'd love to read it.'

'It'd be good to see you if you actually do come down this time. Don't phone unless you're actually in Edinburgh.'

'Sure, I don't want to leave you in the lurch again.'

'Don't mention that,' she snapped.

'I'll let you know when I am there, if I am there. Please take care, you sound awful. If you haven't got over your flu by the end of the week, I'll send you a recyclable carton of orange juice. See you?'

Suddenly Ash felt like taking a pill. Then he considered renewing a library book, except it was only four a.m. and wouldn't be open yet. Instead he did some phone banking. When he loudly said 'yes' to the lady's recorded question whether he wanted to know his balance or not, Helen woke up.

This time, without being asked, he went down on her again. Afterwards she kissed his ear causing such a vastness of pleasure that spread through all his nerves surging like a nuclear kiss detonating over every part of him. He sat transfixed at her feet as if she had just performed a miracle, unwilling to move; to never move from her long, slender toes, but to stay here every day. She touched his ear once more with her tongue as thought she was speaking to him in her body's esoteric cipher.

Eventually she went through to the kitchen and made pork chops with vegetables while he was sent off to buy more wine. During the meal they watched *Withnail and I*. Helen told him of a drinking game where everybody had to imbibe drink for drink all that the characters in the film drank. After that they watched *Children of Men* starring Clive Owen.

Once more, when the film was over, his fingers and tongue were in her. If he lay here between her thighs giving her kisses and nibbling on her, maybe she would never leave him alone. But morning came again and most of the snow had melted.

He said, 'I have to go and see my dad.'

'Now?'

'Takes me two hours to get there. Then two hours back. Come with me on the bus into town and I'll get a bus out to my dad's from Broad Street.'

Helen thought about it for a moment, then leapt up and got dressed.

'There's a bus in nine minutes,' Ash intoned.

'Well get your clothes on.'

He did. He needed to see his dad more than he needed wine, more nasal abrasions, but mainly to rid himself of the fear that he might never see him again.

There was a double decker at the terminus. He started to go up the stairs.

'Not up there,' she said. 'I feel sick.' She plonked herself down on the first seat, in front of which was brown reflective glass. For most of the journey they stared at each other in their reflections, unspeaking. Yet once she started to recognise the buildings and streets a sense of palpable relief came over her.

She put her forehead to the cold glass of the bus window. 'I feel awful,' she moaned.

'If you like I can get the driver to make a detour to your doorstep.'

She laughed and the sound seemed to dispel the despondency of the air at the bottom of the bus.

'God, it's so early,' she said and sighed. 'My back is killing me and I've got to go to GUM for a check-up, but that's not until later on and my back is sore.'

'Man, I thought I moaned a lot, but that must be just in my head. If you like I'll get the bus driver to take you straight to the undertakers.'

A woman across the aisle reading a Danielle Steel novel tittered, and then Helen and Ash laughed together as if for the first and final time.

They said goodbye to each other on King Street. She hugged him, did not kiss him. He looked back a couple of times, saw her sleek in his old black jeans and her silver shoes, the black and white T-shirt about her like wings.

Then Ash went to see his dad.

Chapter Two

Ash's dad was asleep on his end of the sofa, but not for long as Max 2 barked her usual terrified greeting at the sight of Ash. Now dad's moustache had grown thicker, since the last time he saw him, he somehow suited it. He grabbed a mug of tea and asked Ash why he was here.

'I haven't seen you for a bit.'

'You saw me two weeks ago.'

'I just brought Lisa up to see you before they went to LA and Vegas. I was out of my body at the time.'

'No. Why are you here now?'

'I've come to see you. Don't worry, I have no ulterior motives. I just missed you.'

They sat in silence. Then William said, 'Get yourself something to eat and make me a cup of tea, no milk.'

Ash remembered when Helen got so very hot and she became drenched in sweat. She started to panic as she didn't know what was wrong. Ash, with a sense of familiarity, gently blew on her face, which had seemed to help, and she had begun to cool down and had lain in peace for a while.

Ash stupidly put a few drops of milk in the tea, making the liquid look deep brown and murky. He had stopped himself before he put too much in, but it still looked pretty bogging. He took it through, Max 2 darting up the stairs and barking like a terrified fox. Back in the kitchen he got some Cornflakes and came through to the sitting room after perusing his father's boxes and bottles of pills. There were no Jellies. Anyway it was not his intention to snaffle any today, no, not today.

Without setting off the feral beast into a head-ripping bout of barking, he made it to the toilet and back. William unsteadily got to his feet. 'You must have put a milky spoon in my cup.' He went to make another for himself without another comment, but he slowly swept his feet along the hallway and said like a pale shadow of his rage, 'You've left the drawer open and the toilet door shut. How many times do I have to tell you... Oh, I'm sorry it just keeps the heat in that way.'

They both lit up.

'How're you feeling?'

'How the fuck, do you think I'm feeling? I've had the shits since I woke up at six. But, thanks for asking.'

Ash put out his fag then went to get his bag from the steps which set Max 2 off. Ash swore.

William told his son, 'I have to take a pill at ten. Put the telly on if you want.'

'Do you want me to walk Max?'

'Alexa said she would do it. She's a bit later than usual. I'm going upstairs to get washed and changed. Save you from him for a bit.' He stuck the telly on for

Ash as he knew Ash was unfamiliar with the remote. Ash channel flicked and found a found documentary channel, *Eden*, about a guy rowing across the Tasmanian Strait.

William called, 'Can you get me the towels from the dining room? They're on the swivel chair.'

Ash found them and took them up to him while the dog flew to the nearest corner. Ash quickly retreated before he throttled the bark permanently from the mutt. He smoked a couple of fags and had another cup of tea before William came down again with a t-shirt and jumper on, his jeans folded over an arm.

There was a knock on the door. Alexa let herself into the kitchen. Ash said hi to her. She lived two doors down. Her family had lived in Aberdeen before they moved in. He cut her off at the pass.

'Dad's putting his breeks on.' At least Max 2 was consistent and was once again barking insanely.

They both went through and William was fully dressed back in his seat on the couch. Ash told Alexa, 'Max doesn't like me.'

'No. He bloody hates him,' William said.

Alexa took a concerned look at William. 'You're holding your arm funny. Have you had another of your mini-strokes?'

He looked defeated.

'Yes. I think so.'

She managed to wrangle Max 2 into a lead. Ash didn't move lest the dog was too scared to go out.

'I'll take her just now,' she said. 'You'll take her later, Ash, eh?'

'Yes.' He breathed a sigh of relief; at least a break from the dog. Ash started watching TV again. Helen had a little heart tattooed on her shoulder, he said he liked it. She had another tattoo on her thigh — star shaped, edged with grey. I don't like that one, she'd said. Neither did he, but kept it to himself and he had kissed her heart.

Now that he'd woken up and got dressed, taken his pill, and had five fags, William seemed to have cheered up a bit.

Somehow, they got into a conversation about Singapore.

'Your hair was so blonde back then in the sun it turned white. Your mum lost you in the market and was shitting bricks until you appeared on someone's shoulder.'

'I always used to get lost. Especially in Edinburgh.'
William scowled.

'I have to take another pill at eleven, then we can go to ASDA — my second home. I'm waiting for a router, but if it doesn't come soon, we can just go over.'

'Did you get caught out by the petrol panic?'

'I didn't know it was going on until after the fact.'

Before Alexa came back, William told him how he nearly drowned off the coast of Malaysia.

'We were all pissed, big party of us, even some officers. So, bright spark that I am, I went for a swim.

The next thing I knew I was a mile off shore cos of the currents.'

'I nearly drowned for ten fags.' Ash launched into a lengthy spiel, but was caught short by the return of Alexa and the anxious canine, which bounded upstairs as if breathing the same air as Ash was intolerable. Alexa left also.

Ash got up and stubbed out his latest fag in the ashtray beside William. On the table beside it he saw a bonny gold pocket watch.

'That's nice. Did you just get it?'

'No Mum gave it to me.'

'Your mum or my mum?'

'Yours. Helen. I'm going to get a sandwich. Do you want anything?'

'No.' But Ash followed him through to the kitchen. Straight away, through the dining room door, he saw the new sunflower watercolour painting William had recently done. 'It'd look good in a yellow frame.'

'You can have it if you want.'

'Thanks.' But he did not take it that day.

'Do you want these?' His Dad proffered him a hundred John Player Blues.

'Yes, thanks.' Ash put them in his bag. He took out his camera.

'I've some photies to show you.' Before William stopped him, he said, 'that's her.'

'Who?'

'The girl, Helen. And then there's this other one.'
He showed his dad a picture of his sister's wooden
garden chair with an ephemeral hominid shape,
vaporous like a ghost about it.

'What's that?'

'It's a ghost,' he laughed. 'No. I think I was sitting
in the chair smoking and when I got up, I took the
picture the flash must've highlighted the smoke.'

'Can I eat now?'

Ash put away his camera and wandered back
through to the sitting room.

'You up for a trip to ASDA?' William said coming
through unsteadily. 'I need some milk.'

'I'll go over for you.'

'No, it's all right, I want a coffee in the cafe.'

'OK then.'

William got Max 2 leaded and handed his son the
lead. Twice Max slipped out of the collar.

Ash said, 'Shit!'

'Let her get in front of you,' William said and
slipped the collar back over her head. 'Third time's a
doozy.' This time they all got together to the car and
William coaxed the dog into the car eventually. At
ASDA car park they got a convenient space. Anywhere
nearer the shopping centre they would've been blocking
the automatic doors. First stop. The Fag counter. Ash
got some gas and skins. His dad checked a stack of Lotto
tickets.

Ash remembered he needed a new wallet. 'Why don't you sit in the cafe and I'll get you what you need. I remembered I need a wallet.'

'What happened to your old one?'

'Long story,' Ash mumbled.

'I need to go in and get some fish.'

Luckily for Ash the last wallet for sale in the vast shopping centre was hanging on a rack waiting for him. Then he wandered about ASDA not really knowing what he wanted and, if he did, where to find it. A bonny black lassie served him and he went to William at the automatic checkout.

'You're a coward,' he laughed. 'Even I can use these fucking things.'

Finally, they got to the cafe. William got his usual coffee. Ash had a roll and sausage and a hot chocolate.

'Is that all you want?'

'No, but it's what I got.' He almost devoured the roll in two gulps. Oh, that was good. Not as good as when she had kissed his ear. He'd got the gas because the orange clipper she had left had gone out. Even though he had about a hundred and fifty others he regarded this one as special like the Olympic flame that should never be allowed to go out.

When his dad was ready they went back to the car and he asked him to take the dog over the field to the house. Max 2 was as surprised as Ash as they skirted the football pitch and moved toward the primary school. She kept looking back at him as if someone less despicable had replaced Ash the monster. To try and make it up to her for whatever crimes he had obviously committed on the dog, he ran with her over the field back to the house.

'I'd better get a bus soon. I've the mini-shrink to see at 3.30.'

'Who?'

'Simone, the CPN.'

'Oh. OK.'

Yet they had another couple of cups of tea before he left.

'Chilly,' he said to the woman at the bus stop. 'Have you waited long?'

'Five minutes.'

Just then the 21 turned round the bend about the old folks' home.

He had to stop himself from crying the two-hour journey back to his bit.

Chapter Three

At the back of three p.m. he had a date with his Community Psychiatric Nurse. Her name was Simone. She had got married round about the time he started having appointments with her. Damn it, he'd thought wryly, another one bites the dust. She didn't let him wait too long, at least not as long as The Eagles, but even so he twitched and fidgeted and felt the desperate need to pee. Then Simone appeared and took him through to the latest Doctor's office she had borrowed for the day. It was painted bright red with a large framed poster of Barcelona, which caught his eye immediately. Simone enthused about the designer fish tank with a few little, tiddly, fast swimming fish. He thought it was quite an amazing room; it was as homely as if the doctor slept on the examination table.

Ash took his coat off and asked for a tissue to blow his nose.

'How're you doing?' Simone asked.

'On a scale from one to ten. Ten!' he said excitedly.

He told her a little about Helen and that he had actually gone to see his father. Of course he had been slightly drunk, he told her, but to his relief, she didn't hit him with a stick and throw him out the office.

'And I finally went to the Books and Beans poetry night on Thursday.'

'Well done.'

'I read one of my poems, fumbled it a bit, but I enjoyed myself,' he laughed. 'On Belmont Street saw a couple of wimmin; I thought they were mother and daughter, I didn't stay too long after the poetry group, it was about Rilke, a Czeck guy before the First World War. Anyway, I found myself on the street going into the Wild Boar. I sort of like it in there and went in for a pint. Then I went down to Moorings, but didn't stay long and ascended to The Castlegate and saw a pal — Rob the Artist and I dragged him back down to Moorings. In O'Neil's they wouldn't serve me anything but iced water so I left, without Rob, and met this homeless guy, Garth, all hair and beard. I thrust a fiver at him. "Have it," I said. We couldn't get served in one pub, because he had been pilfering drinks from tables, so with him in tow we went to the morgue also known as The Prince of Wales. I ended up in Drummonds getting thrown out for dancing without a license.'

Simone probably thinks I'm still drunk, he considered to himself.

However, he'd avoided telling the whole truth about Helen.

'What does she do?' she asked.

'She's a psychology student.' Lie. She had been a psychology student. Nor did he mention that between them they had consumed about twenty bottles of wine.

If he told Simone she was about the worst alkie he'd met she might get out a slingshot and take out one of his eyes. Or spank him severely. Mmm, he thought Homer Simpson-like on seeing a doughnut.

Ash had missed his last appointment with his newest psychiatrist so he sorted out a new appointment with the doc.

How he hated coming to this fucking health centre. Feels like I've been sitting in that waiting room for the last twelve years. The only thing the waiting room magazines were useful for was having a swift wank in the toilet while waiting for The Eagles to get his finger out and shrink him. Anyway, he'd fired The Eagles a couple of years back and got on with life without a net, until he was given a new doc, a Helen Straven. He thought she was a very kind woman and despite himself he cried about something or other during their last date. He tried to remember what it was that had set him off. When I get home, I'll write a long list, he told himself disdainfully.

Almost an hour had gone by just chatting at Simone. He had her categorised in his mind as a kind platonic pal. If you could call someone who is paid to listen to him once a month, a pal then he supposed she was.

Of course he reconsidered this as he glanced at the swell of her bosom. Were they getting bigger? God, maybe she's pregnant. He didn't know too much about her apart from the fact she was married, used to read

Stephen King a lot, and had seen a UFO. In his head he had used the UFO encounter as an excuse for missing his next appointments with her. I wish I'd seen a UFO, he had pouted at the time. Life is so unfair.

Simone asked, 'Does she smoke?'

'Not pot, a fag or two, she might have had a few puffs but she didn't inhale.'

Simone laughed.

'She even asked me to go into another room when I'd skinned up.'

'I like her already.'

'Not as much as me.'

She wrote a card for a new appointment in May.

'See you then.'

'Take care, Ash.'

He wanted to hug her —friendly-like — but then she would know he was still drunk so instead he pushed himself out the door.

Chapter Four

Alison was late. He thought his sister Veronica's worst aspect of her personality was always being late, but Alison, in his estimation, had stolen the Olympic Gold for lateness. When he'd been in college doing acting he was bawled out extensively by the director, Lynne, until lateness was beaten out of him and he was always early, usually by an hour, which was a bit annoying as the pubs weren't open til eleven. Now Alison was two hours late, and he was on Union Bridge overlooking the Gardens, waiting like a clipper on a street corner. She, however, texted him six or seven times saying she was further down the route on her way, but he didn't get the texts until she finally arrived. At one point, after about an hour, he almost gave up. Ash went to the Wild Boar once a relatively dingy bar which had suited his tastes. These days it had been extensively refurbished. Down in the basement, where he used to sit most Wednesdays when he got his giro was now plastered with TV screens in every booth where smartly dressed folk ate from the refurbished menu. He had a pint there, but didn't enjoy it much. Then, with no idea what else to do, he went back to Union Bridge where a statue of an old king stood watch, clean stone in the sun. There were dwindling crowds of shoppers, folk over the road smoking outside a bar and the buses passing each other within the ballet of their assigned routes.

Recently Alison's latest austerity programme was buying legal highs in the market, especially Black Mamba — a grass-like suspect. She told Ash she would bring a spliff of it down with her and they'd sit in the Gardens while it was still there, before the builders arrived for the glassing of the good, green place that had survived for over a century.

When she arrived at last, smiling, waving from the other side of the street it was almost twilight. Suddenly, as if he had not been irritated by the wait he had to endure, their gloaming tryst seemed a special moment, just the two of them left in the gardens bubbling over with chat in blue dark.

'Some gay guy tried to hit on me while I was waiting,' Ash told her.

'God, this isn't even Hadden Street.'

'What do you mean?'

'It's the new Golden Square. Dogging point for Aberdeen Central.'

'Ohh.'

'A lassie asked me directions to the railway station. She was slender and sweet, in white rush of flowing dress as if she were going to a wedding, but she did have bad acne. In another era I would've called her pizza face. If I'd known you were going to be so effying late I would have personally escorted her.'

'Sorry.'

'It's too late to be sorry, you've already done it,' he laughed. 'So did Rowan get evicted?'

'Not yet. He had a court case and he's got an extension until April. Of course he put Eva back in hospital.'

'When did he get like that? He never hit you, did he?'

'No. I would've hit him back.'

'How's your mum?'

'Still in the old house. She's OK.'

They'd smoked two Black Mambas. Ash was feeling hungry and he presumed Alison did too. So they started along to Belmont Street. Just over the bridge Alison stopped to pull a bottle of Tequila from the pocket of a homeless guy / junkie / person and took a long swig. Ash wondered, what the fuck is she doing?

Yet the guy laughed and said she could have all the Tequila if she wanted it. They obviously knew each other. Ash relaxed against the black railings of the edge of the Bridge. He glanced down as a train off to Inverness started to gain speed on the way to Rosemount Viaduct. He looked back at Alison and the boy chatting to each other. Ash felt like he was in Hermann Hesse's Magic Theatre wondering if this was real or a performance for his benefit. Alison said goodbye to the boy and moved off. The boy looked at him as if he knew Ash but he was pretty sure they had never met. They smiled at each other as if they shared something.

God, I'm on paranoia heights he thought and went after Alison.

'Who was that?'

'Gogs. He was going out with Eva before Rowan.'

'Him?' He shivered with fear. They're coming to get me. 'He's that guy. I hope he realizes there was no penetration involved in our short romance. Are they all going to come out of the cracks and get me?'

She laughed.

Just then they went into Slain's. Since the millennium it didn't seem to have changed a bit. He bought two cocktails — Sloth and Greed. He took her to his usual table, which he hadn't sat at since the fateful Y2K.

'We were sitting here once, my pal Steve and I,' Ash explained, 'getting on with a couple of girls. One of them was on her way to the toilet when she fell down those steps and hit her head and her nose started bleeding so her pal took her to the loo and they were in there for ages. So I reckoned we might as well just go and I tried to get Steve to leave. He kept on waiting for them to come out but, give up, I told him, There's no point hanging about. I almost had to drag him out of here. It was so embarrassing'.

'Let's sit over there,' Alison said. They went to an oak tabled booth. 'When I take out the boys we always sit here.'

Ash agreed that her choice was better. They drank their two deadly sins and looked over the menu. She had pasta and chicken he had ham and eggs and real chips, he hadn't had chips for years. Ash didn't realize how hungry he was until he actually started eating — then the food was gone, and he was still hungry, as if it hadn't existed. He promised himself that he would try to eat more regularly even though it was just a hassle, another bestial human need that took too much thought and effort.

Once he'd finished, he dashed out to the relatively expansive smoking area. The powers that be had even supplied tables for the poor, persecuted, smoking community. He leant against the granite wall of Slain's. Some lassie came up to him.

'Hello we're doing a documentary on people's opinions about the re-development of Union Terrace Gardens.' She looked like a student, another with a movie camera hung back behind her. 'We're looking for people to interview.'

'Yeah? I'd love to.' He had not voted at the referendum on the contentious proposal to redevelop the Gardens. Only about eight thousand people were for it out of population of a quarter of a million. He wondered how many votes the people who wanted to keep it the way it was got. Twenty-three? He had half-expected there to be some street violence. Those brave twenty-three old men, anarchists and radicals (alcoholics and drug addicts) battling it out with hordes of neo-yuppies.

42

'Well,' Ash said, 'I'm with a friend and I'm sure she's got a lot of things to say about it. I'll go and get her.'

He threw down his cigarette even though he knew he could be liable for a fine and that it wasn't very eco-friendly, but this was important, he had thought hastily, and forgave himself. As he walked to the booth he wondered if his views were valid if he hadn't voted. He told Alison about the cameras, expecting her to rush out and express herself, but she didn't budge. He felt sorry for the student who was probably waiting for them both to hold forth.

The bar Slain's was named after Slain's Castle, up the coast from Aberdeen, where Bram Stoker supposedly thought up Dracula. He probably stayed for the afternoon and thought this place is fucking freezing. Ash's sister, Veronica, and one of her mates had taken his daughter there one Summer Holiday. He told Alison about it. 'There's a bit heading to the castle, where there's a sheer drop at both sides. When she walked along past it my heart was in my mouth.

'I know the bit you mean, the boys just rush over it as if it's not there.'

'Oh, God, I hate heights.'

'Let's get out of here. We'll sit outside for a J, I've a bit of that Black Mamba left.' She skinned up with a sense of deftness and surety, yet looked somewhat edgy as they emerged from the pub to the smoking zone. The students were interviewing and filming someone, Ash heard her hiss out a sigh of relief. She noticed small packs of the students prowling along Belmont Street. He and Alison sat in a corner.

'Let's go to The Moorings after this,' Ash said feeling cold and a bit disappointed he hadn't been interviewed. What the hell was wrong with her?

'OK.'

Did she sound unsure? That was why he had met her so they could see the haunted pub. What was bugging her?

They walked the rest of the joint down Union Street, and then turned down past the market towards the pub. A couple of smokers lingered at the doorway. He was about to go in but Alison skirted past them and he had no choice but to sit beside her on some railings and stare at the massive supply boats docked in the harbour at the stars above.

'I wonder if that's Mars,' he said, pointing upwards. 'Oh, come on, let's go inside. I'm cold.'

'No, I don't want anyone to think I'm a prostitute.'

'Don't be silly. I look more like a prostitute than you.' He turned to try and get her to follow him. Her text alert sounded. She had to delete some messages to get the new one and once she'd retrieved it, she wanted to take photos with her camera. Coldly Ash supposed it was a good idea. Then Alison pulled out some Charley Sheen, a brand name for legal cocaine. They snorted a couple of lines from his blue covered journal.

'Can we go in now?'

'I suppose so.'

Thank Christ. Ash wondered if Helen would be here. Suddenly he didn't want to go into The Moorings in case she wasn't there and he'd be disappointed. Even so, both of them reluctantly went in.

It was Karaoke Night. The place was half-dead, except for a few old men in the corners and some Goths with purple hair. The DJ was singing a Johnny Cash song which at first seemed a bit out of place in here until he realised how good the DJ was at singing. He could probably listen to the guy singing all night. Once he'd sung, some thrash punk issued from the speakers and the place almost seemed normal.

Ash said, 'If I go up and do one, will you come and do a song too?'

She didn't answer, so he read between the lines.

Oh great, what fun, we'll just sit here and not speak, as speaking was pointless in the noise. Where was the fucking fun in this? He went back to the bar while she nursed her half pint.

When he had lost his wallet, the last place he recalled being in, was here, one night when he had been looking for Helen. He asked the bartender if it had been handed in. Fat chance, he thought, and he was right. I want to go home; I want a pill. His head wailed above the onslaught of guitars being slowly murdered. He got a pint and split it with Alison.

'I'll walk you to your bus stop. Then I'm going home after this.' He drank the lager quickly, spilling some down his unshaven chin. 'Get a bus, instead of the usual taxi. Treat myself.'

Suddenly Alison began to start getting into Mooring's decor. On one wall a frieze of constellation of stars with Neil Armstrong on a moonlike surface. On the dance floor itself, a white painted line around a corpse removed, sprawled like in the proverbial murder scene. Beyond the black painted wall by the toilet, and the final wall about the dance floor was covered in a mirror. Ash did not know why, but he loved this place. If it had still been a coaching inn, he would have moved in.

He waited at the bus stop with Alison, and then reluctantly got the 19 home. Alison, he decided, was on too much medication or she was so chilled out she slept each night in a chest freezer.

In the house he accidently stepped on one of his cat's tails. She sped off squealing. For no apparent reason he screamed at the cat as if it had been her fault, then clumsily knocked over a coffee. After that he couldn't stop himself from shouting, pointlessly swearing, and he fell to his arse on the carpet and thought about his dad and wept until the anger dissipated.

Chapter Five

It was a wet and grey that day, when Ash set off on a quest to get his passport renewed. For the following two weeks of waiting he hoped, prayed, and would've been willing to sacrifice a lamb if there were one handy for the passport to come. How vividly he recalls that day, in Cults when he wanted to sort it out, that day April deluged.

Thankfully the post office was a giant's tip-toe away from the bus stop and he was out of the wet straight away. Finally, Ash thought, I have found you after so many struggles and hardships and have once dreamed of only this fabled place, finally my quest is fast found and fruitful. Even so, he had not relinquished his grumpy face since the day before. He'd ventured into the city and decided to go to an exhibition of Monets, Manets, a couple of Vetrianos and a Van Gogh. However, for some reason he could not imagine the Gallery was closed. He allowed his grumpy face to linger on into the morning.

The wet grey wet threatened to engulf the world within a deep and vast swimming pool. The wet grey seemed a reflection of his own dark mood.

That day he escaped his house so swiftly, far too swiftly to remember to take his cigarettes with him. The bus was at the terminus and he saw a designer-clothed driver, rolling a cigarette. Ash asked for one and as there was nine minutes to take off, the driver decanted himself from his cab and chatted to Ash under the bus shelter.

The driver, Cammy he said his name was, felled Ash into a conversation. Cammy talked endlessly about his holidays since childhood as if telepathically the driver had gleaned that Ash was going to get his passport sorted.

Also, there was a long poster on the side of the bus advertising a holiday to Tunisia.

'Is the sea really that blue?' he wondered, as if he were a curious small child amazed at the sight, asking his dad.

'Oh, yes.' And the bus driver smiled as if he remembered days of that particular bit of sea. 'When my dad retired, we decide to take him on a World Cruise. We chose the Superior Service Hotel Rate. How we were like Gods, anything we wanted. We even went to the Taj Mahaal; the city around it —Benares — is a right shit hole.' As the driver went on telling Ash all the places he had been to, it seemed to Ash that he had been everywhere, while all Ash had were those days he escaped Culter, if only as far as Toulouse.

Ash said, 'My friend went to Tunisia this year, place was battered with wind and the rain horizontal. A couple of years back my ex took our daughter there, thankfully the Arab Spring hadn't kicked off, a year later I would not have let them go.' Yeah, right, Ash thought. Cammy was going on about Canada, but that was where Ash's mother died. He stubbed out his smoke into the bin and got on board, thanking the driver.

There was a long queue at the post office in Cults, but he had to get his photos first. He'd already filled the form out. The automated photo booth was relatively easily to work and soon he was joining the back of the queue. He looked at the unpleasant reproduction of his skinny face with smoky bruises under his eyes. The old picture on his out of date passport was someone else, a happy head he no longer knew.

Eventually he got to the front to the line, but the woman behind the shotgun sensitive glass told him he should've taken his glasses off for the photos and they were not acceptable.

Bad boy, he reprimanded himself. Go away and do it again. He slumped back to the photo booth. Ash took off his glasses and snapped at the buttons with stressed rigid fingers. This time. No! This time, he repeated to calm himself as he waited in the queue for the second time, this one seemed even longer. Once more the form was wrong. He hadn't filled the signature wholly in the wee box and had to fill in the form for a third time. Has was almost begging the post mistress to accept it now.

Which thankfully she did, apart from the fact that his lips were millimetres open. This time she told him, apart from the lips, everything was acceptable.

Champagne on everyone. As he was leaving, he called back to the postmistress, 'If you want go for a holiday in a couple of weeks, call me.' She didn't laugh; oh it's going to be one of those days. For no other reason than it was next door to the post office, he darted into the Cults Hotel and asked the receptionist if he could get coffee. She gave directions to the dining room. Apart from the staff the place was dead. He got a coffee with a chocolate biscuit —the first time he'd eaten today. He asked the guy who brought over his drink, 'When does the bar open?'

'Eleven,' he said as if Ash had been off planet since decimalisation.

Ten minutes, he said. Ash thought it was probably unwise having a drink today, if he had a drink today it would just increase his depression levels. So he took out the notebook he'd bought in the post office and started writing about what he'd remembered so far today. He knocked back the coffee and left the dry and warm shelter of the hotel. He had won £10 on a scratch card and he needed cigarettes. He didn't much care for the shops in Cults which, as far as Ash could see, were all designed for the rich folks, but along at the end of street near the library was a Tesco.

The wet was seeping through to his long johns, but he struggled on. Of course the Tesco's weren't doing the lotto scratches, so instead of leaving without buying anything, he got some smokes and a half bottle of vodka. He dashed through the soaked air to the Library.

The librarian on duty was a familiar face from Culter Library. He took out a travel book about Berlin and, to make up for missing the exhibition, also took out a tome of impressionist painting. Once more he braved the rain and stood at the nearest bus stop. And waited. At first, he reminisced about Helen, he hoped he would see her again. He had a bag of clothes she'd left behind and she'd told him where she lived. He remembered her hair, coal black, her tattoos, and the cool paleness of her face. After waiting ten minutes all he could think about was how sodden by the rain he was and he took out the vodka and drank a nip.

Another five minutes he told himself, then I'll just walk.

A 201 came out of the rain as if it were defying the rage of an angry god. He got on and found a seat. Thoughts of Helen followed behind and sat down beside him. He went over in his mind how wonderful having had her in his life was; he felt a balm over the pain of his heart as if she had suffered to heal him. Branches of thoughts flitting through in his mind, intertwined and twisted about as if they were the roots of Ygdrassil. Hardly aware of fleeting trees and houses along the way, before he knew it, he was home. Food now, he thought, then pills. He flicked through some of the impressionist paintings, and then tried to look for some Van Gogh's, but the author seemingly had a boner for Monet as one of his pictures was on just about on every page.

Chapter Six

Somehow it was still raining two weeks later when a poor, overworked postal delivery agent rapped on Ash's door. Struggling uselessly into his silk dressing gown he managed, again, to reach the front door without tripping over the cat litter tray. Recently the post never came until midday; the other day he saw a punch-drunk postie delivering his post at two thirty in the afternoon. And there were at least two hundred and forty days till Christmas. Fucking Tories he had thought sadly.

'Hi,' he said to the guy.

The postie still managed a smile as Ash half in and out of his dressing gown and door, signed the proffered piece of paper and accepted the slim unassuming blue envelope. He swore at himself for wishing it had come the day before when he was in a good mood and not today when he'd barely slept and had an unnerving foreboding sloshing like sewage in the back of his head. Almost as an afterthought, the postie gave him his real post. A call for funds for overworked and suicidal recorded PPI voiceover artistes promoting their campaign: Why Don't You Talk to Us. Ash vaguely wondered if he should give the postie a tip. A hug? That would be a bit out of place especially with the dressing gown about his legs.

'Thank you,' Ash said. It'll have to do. He presumed they still got paid.

He shut the door as the postie went off into the bleak Wuthering Heights-ish day. He sat on his bed. 'Her Britannic Majesty...' That's nice of her, he thought. God look at the picture, I look like a fucking dusty gargoyle. He put the passport on the table by the bed. Stood up, paced about the table, eyes firmly locked on the red imitation leather cover. He sat down and picked it up again. He looked at the pictures on the pages — oh that's cool. He put it down again and managed to escape its lure by making a well-earned coffee. He put on the radio; a strangely amusing documentary about kissing was on.

Helen didn't like kissing much. He wondered what she was doing and if she was still alive. He'd gone to her student flat with a bag of her clothes, but she wasn't in. Somehow, he wasn't surprised, almost relieved. But, if he hadn't taken his camera with him, afterwards, he might have fallen onto the road and let whatever vehicle nearest to him, crush him to gore and pulp. Instead he took some photos and went to Veronica's flat in Bridge of Don. Why does that seem such a long time ago now? He wondered, and then with the coffee, went back to his vigil with the passport. He smoked and drank coffee while the cats stalked him. They'd been on hunger strike as their cat food wasn't made with the correct combination of gravy, rabbit and vegetables and several days' worth of it was rotting in the kitchen. He assured them that once Lisa's mum called he'd get them something more palatable. He went to the window, the curtains still undrawn, went to open them and saw cops talking to his neighbour. He sat back down again considering the consequences of this, if any. Luckily, before he had seen the neighbour banged up, his girlfriend thrown out into the street and a new, golden summer of middle-agedness open, the phone went.

'Hello, it's Rachael, Lisa's mum.' She added ironically, 'Lovely day.'

'Yeah, great, apparently ducks like this kind of weather. I just think they're not on enough medication and need their eyes tested.'

'You'll never guess what happened to me.'

'You're right, I don't know. My usual mindreading devices are off. You got drunk? Got married? I don't know give me a clue.'

'Well my chums took me out for a meal cause of my fiftieth and my sister told me to dress up and I got a pair of heels.'

'Never do anything families tell you to do,' Ash said, with a sinking sense of prescience.

'Well we were out and enjoying the meal and I went to go to the toilet. It was a bit slippy on the floor, and I went right over on my back.'

'Oh my God I'm sorry. What happened?' Thinking that she'd broken her back. Who the fuck's going to do my ASDA shop now?

'Anyway, I'd dislocated two fingers in my hand. They were all saying to go up to A&E. But it was Saturday and I wasn't going up there. I said I wasn't going to let it spoil my night and soldiered on. I went to A&E next day and they gave me some gas and air. Remember, like when Lisa was born'.

They both laughed.

'The nurse was good, but I still screamed when she snapped the fingers back in place. So much for being fifty.'

'Oh god,' Ash said. 'It's your birthday, when? Saturday? Ahh Sunday. I don't have anything for you.'

'No. Remember you gave me that CD.'

'Oh, yeah, but.' Then suddenly out of nowhere Ash started crying. He could hear the portcullis going down in her head.

'I don't know. I want to go and see Dad, but the cats want food and I need a shower. I don't know what to do. I don't know what's important.'

'Have you been taking your medication?'

'No. I took them all on Friday with some sleeping tablets. I don't remember what happened. And I was all paranoid thinking I'd screamed and shouted at you or Veronica or Dad.'

'Ash, calm down. Go down to the GPs and ask them for some.'

'They won't give me any, I've tried before.'

'Well then call your nurse.'

'They're no use. They're always so busy.'

'Just call her, don't lose it at her just explain what happened. It's not like they're going to section you.'

But Ash wouldn't stop crying.

'I'll call you back in a minute.' Rachael hung up.

Breathe or something, he told himself and grasped a cigarette, had sucked half of it into him before she called back.

But he was still crying.

'You've got to get some pills, Ash. You can't see Lisa when you're like this.'

I'll be all right, Ash was thinking. Fuck him, fuck him next door. He did this to me. No, he argued, I did this to me.

'Just call your nurse and text me tomorrow if you're still up to seeing us.'

'OK.'

'Bye.'

'Yeah.'

For a while Ash wandered about with his passport until the cats had demented him enough to brave the day. As he wandered down to the Spar he remembered that the London Marathon, where a woman had died, had been on at the weekend. Twelve years ago, he said to himself, that's when I did the play in London. He decided not to go into the shop just yet and went past the chippie and the pub down toward the river. At first, he felt a sense of real joy. Old friend, old friend. The water loud and falling fast. Then he saw the outcrop of rock where he had been sitting when some vicious cunt lobbed a boulder at his head. He looked up and was startled by the wood pigeons. He saw the grey flare of the water. Suddenly suicide seemed possible. Not now, but whenever. Here. On a day like this. Probably hurt a bit, but I probably deserve it. He turned back to go to the shop and the tears almost swamped him again. OK, other people alert. He did this every week. It's cool.

There were the same vegetables that Helen insisted he buy, marked down in price. He considered buying them, but didn't think there was much point as he probably wouldn't eat them. The familiar face of the antipodean wifie was on the till.

'Where are you from again, Australia or New Zealand? I know I've asked before...' Ash asked.

'New Zealand.'

'I knew that. I've family in Perth.'

'That's £24.90.'

'£24.90. Just like that.' He laughed. 'I got my passport today. Only £600 to Perth. At least when I get there, I won't have to buy any groceries.'

He made her laugh. Maybe it won't be such a bad day after all.

While the cats were wondering what new poison he had set down for them to sup, he went on Facebook to tell the director of Calendar Girls that he wouldn't be able to turn up for the audition.

Ash could just about figure out emails and blogs, but Facebook seemed, well, basically weird and the fact that one day he suddenly had all these friends, why didn't they just phone him up?

Somehow though, something caught his eye from his cousin in Australia about her dad, Mickey, dying thirty-six years ago to the day. He hadn't thought about Uncle Mickey for years, had a vague memory of an old photo, and when Ash was a boy, he'd sent him a gold tie clip and cufflinks with a map of Australia on them. He did a figure in his head. I was ten then, I remember that day, or I remember Mum being so upset.

Did it mean anything that by accident he had noticed the message on Facebook, which he'd mainly avoided using, and getting the passport on the same day. Well, he decided, it had to mean something or at least only to himself.

He remembered that Mickey had been a painter and decorator and he'd suddenly died in his forties on the ladder. It could mean:

A) (As he looked at the badly painted doors, walls and ceiling) that he should paint the flat.

B) That he could avoid painting his flat by getting on a bus to the bus stop where the bus to the airport left from, getting on a plane to London and then another plane, or three, and going to see his family in Australia. Right now.

C) He was beginning to see connections in everything as he was probably breaking down.

Of course, A was the most sensible of the three, but he'd been putting off painting his house for the last ten years and, despite the call from the Great Beyond, he didn't whip open the can of white emulsion and begin He probably could've got to Perth, spent a long summertime there, come back by boat, yet when he got back would still be sitting here for years and still not paint this fucking place.

He tried not to think about it too much and had a shower. He realised he'd been sitting in the house for a week. That was the point — he'd been trying to get out more when he met Helen. Now he was back to the same old same old, sitting, doing nothing. He remembered Helen's bag of clothes in the hall cupboard. I suppose I don't need a passport to try and find her. Try and find her? But, could he put himself through all that? That was what he was hiding from, sitting here, thinking, thinking, and thinking. Oh fuck, he thought. Then he went to bed.

Unfortunately, he couldn't sleep.

He considered what Rachael said about calling his nurse. He knew there was no point, but he did it anyway. Got the fucking answerphone. Right I've got to do something and he realised he was just walking about from room to room while the cats circled, followed him, were there at his feet, and at his hand, as he parted the curtains briefly. There was a medical term for pacing about without being aware of it. Fucking annoying-ism.

He sat on the toilet and started reading *The Storyteller* by Alan Sillitoe. This guy knew, Ash said to himself. How stories are everywhere, but just as you get a handle on them, they fly off and you can't reach them, you can't grab them and hold them and let them fall out of your mouth like God was speaking for you.

Then one of the cats came to the door of the toilet and looked at him.

'What?'

The days, then the months went by, each one followed as a string of forgotten days. The months echoing the rain in him, the months of mist that seemed sheeted on the dusty green of trees beyond the front window, all alike as if the Earth was in mourning. He read, wrote his journal, saw his daughter, and read some more. But, he didn't write, he lived in abject fear of the computer after he had tried to find out what had happened to a woman called Jacs he had known in Glasgow. She had given birth to his son; on a website he had found his son's obituary. He thought he might have wept, but he didn't. Numbness fell over him, beneath the medicated pillows of his head. A great rage formed and grew within him. He stopped calling folk so much, sleeping so much, and didn't eat. He wanted to run. He wanted another adventure into the unknown. But now he was a coward, and he saw only barriers to his desires. After a while, it became easier, once more he got used to the emptiness of the world about him, got used once more, to his game of loneliness and though he struggled, he began to write.

Chapter Seven

Chapter one — where our hero smiles for the first time in years, dances, is thrown out of a pub, and then performs a few sneaky kisses on thin air.

I hadn't been to the monthly poetry group in Books and Beans before though I had been thinking about going for about five years and every time the last Thursday of the month passed, I would flagellate myself wildly. I took along 'Song upon the Flame', just in case. I had forgotten the routine. Upstairs of the cafe and bookshop, clutching a coffee, I made my way through to a seat at the back, fortuitously beside the sci-fi section. The place was humming with conversations and the light in the room was bright and warmly lit. Slowly people began to settle. On the row beside me was a couple of guys chatting away to each other, in the seat next to me sat a lassie, quite tall looking with a long beige coat and hiking boots. I wondered if she was the fabled Rowena who wrote a lot about King Arthur and his ilk who I heard about at the odd group when I had mentioned one of my own stories in the same vein. Soon proceedings got started.

I tried quite successfully to focus on the tale about the poet Rilke and enjoyed the reading of the poet's work. Halfway through, a well-dressed but harassed looking guy came in with a laptop and sat on a stool by the counter in front of me. I began to drift away and looked along the rows of sci-fi and fantasy books. Got that one. And those two and, none of L. Ron Hubbard's ten-part trilogy of arse wipe. He looked with certain adoration at Stephen Donaldson's epics. He read them all at least three times. Only two years, six days and a few moments, until the final instalment of the latest Tom Covenant saga coming out. Oh, happy day.

The latecomer in front of me went forward and took centre stage. I managed to easily focus on the guy's voice and saw more of Rilke's poetic identity. The leader of proceedings, Arthur, apologised but the speaker had no more time and next there were to be some of the gathering's poems. Arthur asked me if I wanted to read one. I said I would. I thought Rapunzel Wizard read out the best one. Me and the lassie beside me were next. I read the title poem of *A Song upon the Flame*. Didn't stutter and performed it quite well, afterwards Rapunzel and the guy beside me gave me an appreciative look. I made my way downstairs once the group was done and rushed to have a smoke, Rowena followed behind. When I lit up she made an exasperated noise. But I decided to disregard it and instead followed a couple of lassies who had been the first to escape into a pub opposite. I got a pint and saw the women settling into seats at the back. I got a seat by the window considering whether or not to speak to them, but realised I didn't have the bottle. I had another pint then left dejectedly. I walked down to the Moorings but that place was pretty dead and I didn't want to hang about so I went up to a pub at the corner of Union Street. Rob the Artist was there reading *The Times*. I was glad to see a familiar face. I chatted away to him. Told him about the Rilke poems and signed the copy of *Song upon the Flame* to him.

'I've given one to most of my friends; you're my friend so this is yours.'

Somehow, I managed to drag him down to Moorings and bought him some of the lager I call amnesia brew, telling the barman that I'd lost a couple of hours the last time I drank it. Made the barman laugh. We got a table a where Chinese woman and pixie short girl were talking beside us. I didn't at all resist the urge to speak to the Chinese girl, but pixie lady asked me what I was doing and told me her friend was married. I apologised a couple of times and smiled at Bob and shot myself in the head with nicotine stained fingers. I felt an urge to leave. So we traipsed up to O'Neill's near where I'd started from in Books and Beans. The barmaid wouldn't serve me a drink but poured me a pint of water — was she being sarcastic or obtuse? I wondered if the girl knew how much money I'd invested in here back in the day when I used to projectile vomit across Union Street. I took a few sips of the water, angry, and decided to leave. As I went out the door, I bumped into Phil, a homeless guy with a mass of hair and the same clothes he was wearing the last time I passed him in the street months ago.

'D'ya wants a fiver? D'ya wants to go for a drink?' I said, as if I'd known Phil all my life though I'd never spoken to him before. We went to one round the corner. She behind the bar wouldn't serve me.

'Whyni?' I complained. She pointed at Phil. 'He's been banned for drinking from other people's drinks.'

I turned and set out, Phil in my wake. We frog-marched to The Prince of Wales and we got served this time. We sat quietly. I couldn't think of a single thing to speak to Phil about so I waffled at him intensely until I decided to go off again along the cobbles of Belmont Street to the last bar on the right. Not long after, I had started dancing on the empty dance floor and falling over, a gracious barman asked me to leave. I apologised and left, got into a taxi. I don't know what I did when I got back to my bit, but I must have gone off planet for a while.

Chapter 2 — Our hero finishes work, feeds the cats and forgets to look for a job, again.

For a while people started to neglect their duty of care towards me and stopped treating me with their obligatory respect and deference. I concluded that my decision to run as a local community councillor should be rescinded as these, 'my peers and contemporaries', obviously no longer needed the sacrifices, effort and time I bestowed upon them.

I delivered the last copy of The Sun into the last letterbox; my musings came to a halt.

'Only seven thirty a.m. and my day is done,' I thought, with surprise.

I sighed. Tomorrow was the Sundays, bent double like old beggars under sacks. I took out my Guardian, just a slip of a thing these days, and walked back to my bit reading the bullshit. My shoelaces like four snakes on hunger strike trailed behind me trying impetuously to trip me but failing pathetically at every attempt.

An attack of cats greeted me at the door. Eva, the sprightly three-year-old, dashed into the morning without her breakfast. Emily, tortoiseshell, nineteen summers young, followed me like a loyal servant to the cat bowl and eyed me with round, greedy and yellow greens. I opened the can I'd carried since first thing in the morning.

Emily ate. I said afterwards, 'Well make me a coffee'. But she went to sit on the red armchair where a shard of sunlight remained.

I tried to read the paper. But, after smoking three cigarettes, I lost track of the words.

'All propaganda and balderdash.' I threw it down at the side of the ebony sofa as I lay there.

For a while I looked up at the smoke-dim ceiling and decided for the thirtieth time since last weekend to paint it. But I felt the pain in my back, and the endless screaming of tinnitus.

I tried to block it out by making up buzzwords in my head:

50 Shades of Puce.
The Psychiatrist's Pneumatic drill.
The Homeopath's Heartache.
No Country for Middle-aged Men.

I supposed I should write it all down, but once all the desk drawers in my head were stuffed, more buzzwords and phrases came along, drifting into the teeming filing cabinets in my head. The next buzzwords came along, then another, like that spider.

I put on the radio. The theme tune of *The Archers* came on so I stuck it off straight away.

The first PPI compensation call of the day banged me back into reality. I let the phone ring out. A thud of the letterbox sprang me into action.

I'd been recycling three or four times a day to get me out on Saturdays. I sent the lonely Scientologist's letter straight to be pulped, unopened. I even forgot to tear off the stamp.

I suddenly felt like going to Edinburgh and bombing Scientologist HQ. They'd been trying to communicate since 1980. Briefly I considered starting my own wee cult. But I realised it would be too much effort.

I took my morning dose of Uncle Depressants. Then took tomorrow's too and sat on the step by the front door.

Chapter Eight

A month passes, two, then another, already dust was gathering on the passport somewhere in a drawer. If he thought about it, it was only to regret the energy and money he'd wasted on the wee bits of papers and bonny pics he would never now probably use. Apart from his cats everything seemed to get further and further away from him. Each day he told himself that he should pop out to Dyce and see Dad, he had appointments with the Mental Hygienist, Simone, but he missed about four, either cancelled them or just didn't turn up. When three months — since he'd last seen Helen — had passed, months filled with torpor and TV, trips out to get the cats food or trips down to the library to take out books he'd not read, still he had barely seen a soul, apart from Rachael and Lisa. Yes, he called William. Dad sounded so much mellower on the phone, but Ash knew if he'd been Skyping his dad he wouldn't feel as content actually seeing how frail he was. His sister, Veronica, called, mainly to tell him how busy she was and what the buzz was in her back garden — the hydrangeas are fair taking off. Right. Lovely. Ash could barely stop himself from hanging up some days. He'd call Martha, the poet in her crystal city, but he almost always regretted it, before and after he did it. Ash would think about the conversation, thinking after all these years, do I know her? Am I the same with everyone? He filled the days with movies and TV shows on computer websites, unable to move away from the mouse. Clicked on the next show or film, the contents of the film being sucked into an empty black hole. Then after that, the next and the next, filling the screen the actors' lives reflected in his glasses and grey crusted eyes. Flicking, clicking, over and over the next and the next, as if he were searching out some obscure idea in CCTV footage. Searching perhaps, for a little truth, someone to chat with, but just these twenty-four / seven images of emptiness clogging up his head and soul, denying existence to his soul. He would always get by just watching another then it was to find some excuse to get out and escape Culter. But there was always cat food to get, and gas, yes there was the TV license, and food. Fucking food. It drove him insane, the demands of his body, to go up and down to the Mace day after day and coming back with nothing he wanted.

One week, around about the time of the Olympics, Veronica turned up just as he was about to pack up his rage like a tent and leave it there in a shed, or cupboard, until his next camping trip, but he hadn't sealed it away too well, or hidden it properly, in the silent shed. He and Veronica were having their day with Lisa, which was normal, once a year, during summer. They were going to get a pizza and… well, that was about it. Lisa liked pizza. Veronica used to make fine pizzas, but she was always too busy these days, what with William and Ronnie, he seemed in need of more care than dad. Needs a bloody minder what with some of the things he comes out with, Ash thought as Veronica came in the front door. Almost at once the metaphorical tent of rage spilled out of the cover, out of the shed, and took off on a really strong gust of a wind. She sat in the back garden, instantly knowing it would piss him off, and started reading a stolen GPs copy of the *Reader's Digest*. Hypocrite, he thought. The ding-dong soon started.

'What the hell are you doing here? If you've just come to read then you can just do it in your car.'

That started it.

'Don't you start shouting and swearing at me.'

'Swear at you, I'll rip your fucking throat…'

'Right that's it. I'll be in the car if you still want to see your daughter.'

He threw his howls of rage at her like sugar free custard pies and slammed the door behind her.

Lisa. Lisa, he thought for what seemed an hour, as if the word could make him better.

He called Veronica's mobile.

'Hello, hello. Have you left yet?'

'What?'

'Have you left?'

'No, I'm just outside your house.' He looked out the window but couldn't see the car, as if some joker had covered the window with a picture of the road outside, with all the life missing from it. But he trusted Veronica if she says she's there she must be there. She came up behind him flinching as he locked the door.

'Can I use the toilet?'

He let her in and dashed to the sanctuary of the car, avoiding speaking to the old couple who must've heard the shouting and were trying to see what was going on.

Veronica had a five-minute conversation with them about her blooming hydrangeas. He almost hit the windshield with his head trying not to piss tears from his eyes.

Come on, come on, come on. We're going to be late.

Veronica eventually got in the car, but before they'd even driven twenty meters down the hill, Ash was letting rip. The scythe of his words though was blunt, all the blame he cast at her with yelling and expletives seemed to fall on her like soft rain. He tried all the old arguments, brought those same incidents that he'd tried to stab her with over the years. But today the knife was a dummy. He tried something new, her childlessness — this would do it and they'd both die in the crash as she tried to attack him and the car spun out of control, but he might as well have been offering her a mouldy biscuit. Her face stretched out onto the road. He started the old wounds bleeding, but now they bleed very little, could easily be brushed away like a solitary tear. He would have floods, but he didn't get it.

He wasn't surprised when she swore; he could see it coming, but not what came next. He wasn't expecting this.

'Get out of the car.' She swung over to the side of the road. 'Just get out of the fucking car.'

He stayed sat. 'I've just won a fiver. I wagered myself that I could get you to say the F-word before musshie season and the C-word by Christmas.'

'Well you've lost your bet, you cunt!' She swung round at him. 'Just get out of the car.'

Inside he was apologising to himself. What am I doing? What am I doing? I just want to see Lisa, why am I such a pathetic little man?

'Oh, come on, Vers, I was just bored, we said we'd be there at two.' All his mannerisms and voice changed in an instant, an actor daddy in control. He told himself to try not to kill the designated driver.

'Vers? Where is it we're going?'

'Gordon's.'

'Right.'

Slowly she made her way back into the traffic and they drove toward Gray's School of Art and the Robert Gordon's Sports Complex where Lisa was involved in a holiday club. Once there they made their way to the large gymnasium on the bottom floor where Lisa and a tribe of about one hundred summer orphaned primary schoolers were rehearsing for the group show. Ash saw a poster for it, everyone was invited, oh, that'll be quite a good thing to do. He craned his head around the gymnasium door and finally saw Lisa, older, it seemed, than the others as she picked her way over bags and crossed legs. With a look of relief at Ash, she made her way towards them.

He wanted to hold her, but for her sake he'd keep it cool.

'What's this about a show…?'

'Hello, Auntie Veronica.'

'Were you going to do something?' Veronica asked.

Skirting the question, Lisa said, 'Those boys are doing break-dance,' and pointed in the vague direction of the open door of the gym.

'Look', Auntie Veronica said, 'they are climbing walls all the way up the building. Do you want to do some climbing?'

To Ash's relief, Lisa said no in response. The last time the three of them had gone on the climbing walls at the Extreme Sports Club by the beach he had shit himself. Literally.

By default, they went to the cafe a floor above, he bought them juice and he a healthy sugar-based cup of coffee while they watched the summer tribes of kids down below in the gym rehearse their acts for the show. As usual afterwards, they went to ASDA and Ash did his weekly shop with lots of help from his daughter. Veronica had gone off somewhere, probably to stick needles in a voodoo doll of Ash, so they trailed through the desolation of products and, by increments, his trolley filled. He thought, somewhat perturbed, that he might be getting too many chocolate biscuits. But, he rationalized, I have a Visa card and I know how to use it

At the checkout Veronica returned, like Gandalf always turning up at exactly the right moment and surveyed his trolley.

'Did you get pizza?'

'Oh—' Ash mumbled so they all traipsed back from the queue to where the variety of fresh pizza was on display. He remembered the plan was pizza in the garden. Oh, not the garden ritual again, he thought and imagined the three of them hunched outside on his patch of green eating their food in the 'sunshine' of 'summer' like a small family of crows on a telegraph pole. He really didn't want to drag Lisa back to his bit, cat-stink heights. He remembered that Veronica had been redecorating her study, he had said before that he'd go round and see it although he hadn't, perhaps they could do that, he thought, slightly excited by the idea. Veronica though was having her regular dose of road rage so the thought went out of his head

'You're so selfish and you don't even know it,' Veronica had said during his earlier fit of apoplexy. As if he didn't. I've been selfish and mean all my life and I have no way of knowing how to stop. I'm a pathetic, cruel little schizo. He felt the voice of William in his skull when she'd spoken pleading with Ash to help and visit him. Ash scowled at himself in the side mirror, hearing the voice and knew it was too easy to ignore and he would just go on smoking and smoking, clicking and clicking, to shut out the voice, that wasn't real anyway. Finally, some Audi let them out onto the roundabout.

Back in the back garden, where the mood of the heat and sunlight had changed and seemed to be healing the pain between sister and brother, they ate their pizza. Not like scrounging, unhappy crows, but as if they were on the side of a vast open air swimming pool, their eyes open to the cornucopia of life, the grass splashing, the birds like high divers swooping about them, and the familiar sight of the garages like bored faced lifeguards up on their airy step ladders.

To close his special daddy day, one once again ruined by his mood, Veronica and Lisa surfed the web for laptops and phones; he had to quell his rage for a while so he paced about from garden to bedroom, wondering why they bothered as they were probably not going to buy anything. A phone for fucking £400 and they call me crazy, he thought.

Lisa and Veronica left him at the doorstep; she put Lisa in the car and ran back over to admire the white roses on the bush climbing up the wall. She gave him a hug as if that could melt the shame in him. He watched them drive away, went inside, locked the door, drew the curtains, and then watched a film, then another, and just one more after that, then slept for two days, but woke up angry again.

Chapter Nine

In the past, Wednesdays, for Ash, had always seemed to be the best of days, he received his benefits, cast adoring glances at the vibrant redhead at the apothecary when he picked up his pills, and wandered down to the River Dee to sit in his chosen suntrap, read, wrote, whiled away the time until he had to go to pay off his tick. Now Fridays had taken the place of a busy Wednesday, these days the benefits he got were paid into his Lloyds account, and instead of going down to the banks of the river Dee, feeling the sun on his face, he would invariably dash back to his bit as if he had something worth returning for. The redhead in the pharmacy who had got up the stick was off on her maternity leave. Nothing felt the same; nothing seemed filled with the same sense of contained excitement.

William's Wednesdays seemed to have lost their allure also. He never went to his art classes anymore, not since he had broken his hip. Also, he hardly drove at all —except maybe to get his Navy pension from the post office or to take Mad Max for a walk along the river Don. As he fondly reiterated, ASDA cafe had become his second home. He knew most of the staff by name. Though frail and slow, William kept to his routines.

Even though Ash had the mini-shrink on the cards for the day, and he'd been awake for a day and a couple of nights, there was something in the air, that sun bright yearn of morning as there had been in May. Synchronicity seemed to be powering the day. Before he switched off the morning news marathon, he heard that the Council had decided to change their fickle minds about the modernisation of Union Terrace. Perhaps somewhere Ash was unaware of wheels grinding into motion, for a fortuitous meeting with Helen on the 21 to Dyce. He was barely a moment or two at the bus stop when his bus arrived. High up on the front seat of the top of the bus Ash watched the summer roll by reaching all the way to Dad;s house.

Mad Max greeted Ash with the usual deafening fear and swiftly sought a place of sanctuary, under some coats or perhaps the downstairs toilet. William had his back to him standing at the stove obviously cooking some liver and onions by the succulent aroma issuing over his shoulder.

'It's only Ash, Max,' he said, as if Ash was in and about every other day and the quivering mutt should've got used to him by now. It had been three months since his last visit but it felt just like yesterday. Ironically it seemed Dad had been waiting for him to get there so they could have their lunch. Ash never phoned in advance to say he would put in an appearance as William would invariably tell him not to bother coming out. So Ash used this stealth tactic, yet it didn't surprise him at all when William told him, 'I knew you'd be out today.' Did he feel it in his waters or in some past life memory of a war wound? Did he have a side line as a Psychic on the web?

His dad's moustache seemed displayed upon his lip like a well-earned but tarnished medal as he turned to Ash, with his palpable relief that Ash wasn't on a bender and he would have to endure an hour or two of mental torture. At once, as he saw that William wasn't as gnarled and near death as his sounded on the telephone, Ash realized that voice of pleading in his head was not William's voice but his own, and he was relieved.

Ash took the dog for a walk over the wide featureless field outside the front of the house, he skirted quickly past the ring of 'standing stones', past a sparsely occupied set of swings and a solitary slide up toward the nursery. He narrowly avoided the more upmarket area and reached the far side of the field. He and Max, like old lovers making up after a vicious fight, ran back to William's house and reached the door before for the first storm cloud to released its surprise that day.

For a while a companionable peace fell over the two men as they sat with their mugs of tea and ashtrays. Both sat for a while reading. Then as they both reached the end of a chapter together, they laid their books aside.

Ash asked, 'Do you still have a nap at lunchtime?'

'Yeah I do, that's a good idea.'

'I'll go over to Associated Dairies and get some stuff and a coffee.'

'Come back at twelve thirty and wake me. I have to take a pill.'

By this time the rain had stopped. He did a bemused waltz about the aisles of the supermarket trying to find something he could bear to eat. Dyce School nearby was on a lunch break and he was amazed at the lines of kids at the cafe or like a horde of locusts at the fag counter buying up sandwiches and packets of crisps. Yet by the time he had circumnavigated the supermarket, bought the cats' food and a fancy microwave dinner, all the children had vanished as if the lino covered floor hid a subterranean level where they scoffed, smoked and spoke to each other on mobile phones.

With the rain at his back Ash reached the shelter of his dad's bit and Max duly woke William from his pinched, pixie-faced slumber.

'Make yourself some soup.' He showed Ash how to light the gas ring directing his hapless hands. The afternoon went well enough, they talked, and seemed to laugh a lot more than usual. They walked Max down by the River Don and, at four, ate liver and onions, mash and chopped carrots in front of a *Countdown* free television screen until they were stuffed to the gunnels.

Ash felt a moment of triumph as he stood at the bus stop. I haven't stolen or necked his sleeping tablets, started weeping and told him I love him, put milk in his tea, or cut his throat. He threw down a half smoked cigarette as the bus turned the corner. When he got home a couple of hours later he felt jetlagged as if he had been away so long and suddenly his life felt new again.

Chapter Ten

The day before Ash's birthday, Helen sent him an obscure Facebook message. He darted one back to her asking if she was up for a home visit, then he half hopelessly batted a couple more messages back at her. Then nothing. Before he began checking Facebook every five minutes, he switched off his computer and listened to *Poetry Please* until medication time and fell into the futility of his broken bed.

Even so, the lack of Helen did not spoil the advent of his forty-seventh year. Lisa and her mum came for the usual Saturday visit. That day they went to Alford. Ash vaguely recalled going to Alford at least once before. Thirty years ago, perhaps to the day. That day there were a lot of stinking steam engines in a field of mud. He remembered he had thought at the time. Why are we here? I think I'm going to throw up! Oh, another photograph!

He clunk-clicked beside Rachael, the customary steering wheel before her.

They drove along a new road through the 'shire, past a loch and a bird sanctuary, through the ever-steepening vista of hills, sun clad and tanned, tattooed with sheep and highland bulls. The car hefted down through a valley and before they knew it, they were in the small village of Alford's driving down its main drag.

What a day it was, like no other, uninvited into the summer of rain. Before their adventure in Haughton Park they went to a subdued bar with the bare window beside their table and they shared a meal.

Rachael and Lisa had sandwiches but didn't eat their greens or the potato chips on the plate. He had steak pie and steamed vegetables.

Mum said she loved Alford, said she would live here if she could. He didn't say that, though he thought she probably could, but she loved her job, or so she said, and now Lisa was in Big School it diluted her option of leaving Aberdeen and living here.

Then they went to Haughton Park and played on the swings and slides and climbing frame, and watched the miniature train flitting in and out of the foliage, blurring so slowly by. Ash took a lot of photos as he and Lisa ran and jumped over tree stumps taking a whirlwind tour of the park and back to Rachael for a spot of tennis.

Afterwards they went to the steam engine museum. The stinking jumped up tractors had their own museum now instead of a muddy field. There was an old British army tank out in the courtyard. He stood in front of one of those old police boxes as Rachael took a few pictures of Ash posing in blue like a bemused Timelord who remembers to smile just in time.

Back in the centre of Alford, coffee and cakes were on the cards. Firstly, they went into the nearest. It was a bit of an upmarket minimalist charity shop with over-priced tat, cookbooks from the thirties, and clothes on a rack that Rachael flicked through absently. But, as soon as they went in, Lisa had seen the paltry offerings on the cake tray, she dragged her parents out and chased them across the road as if she were herding a couple of lost sheep to another cafe. At once, inside the door, Ash espied meringues. He loved meringues. He thought that perhaps he could change his name by deed poll to Mr Meringue. These meringues seemed the King of Kings of meringues, sizeable as Sylvester Stallone's right fist. He grudgingly permitted Lisa a dab or two of cream. Rachael looked away (from the temptation of the meringue) and, to his relief, said she didn't want any.

He asked Rachael to drive slowly back to Culter as he knew the two of them wouldn't stay long once they got him home in the car. He put on the CD they'd given him for his birthday and discussed their favourite tracks on the compilation while about the car the 'shire ran at its own pace, the woods and the waters, as horses stock-still galloped by them.

The cat stench and stink from his wheelie bin of the many mice that Emily and Eva had eviscerated greeted them at the back door.

'I've had such a good day,' he told them and thanked them for his presents. 'I'll buy a carpet for the bedroom with the money I got,' Ash said, as he walked them back to the car.

'We'll be back on Monday, mind,' Rachael assured him. He kissed the top of Lisa's ginger head of hair. As he usually did, he raced back to the house and waited at the front window to wave at them and throws a couple of kisses. Then they were gone, driving away for another hundred years or so until the following Monday.

Chapter Eleven

The Friday after Ash took an overdose of sleeping tablets, he found himself in his sister's yellow car on their way to Stonehaven. Somehow, calmly and clearly, he explained what had happened. But he could not find the words to explain the loss he had felt in that moment, the moment between not even considering taking an overdose of sleeping tablets and then stuffing them down his maw. That moment before the world was not over and he felt he had chapters of his life ahead, albums worthy of love, songs to sing, then it had vanished like snow in a brisk thaw and, as he sat in her bright yellow car racing like a comet to the sea, he could literally feel banality bricking up all the doors and windows in his life.

She sat beside him listening, waiting for him to tell his tale. Patiently. Willingly, because he wasn't screaming and shouting and blaming it all on her. Of course there wasn't much that she could do but drive and take it in and drive.

Ash loved the road to Stonehaven, over the River Dee where plodding anglers, stock-still in the summer sunshine, played. Sweeping back up the valley past the ostrich farm, almost on the way to Storybook Glen, but not taking that particular turning, heading along the other way and racing past a few odd couple of houses at the sides of the road. Taking in the obscure names that signposted single track roads to farmhouses, then sweeping on further and further to the sea, he always anticipated the incongruous site of an old RAF jump jet outside a business park. And soon, somehow, laughter found itself back into the car, the sight of the sea swept into the ache of his eye, as if seeing the still blue water was a memory of a surprise of childhood.

They negotiated their way through the placid streets of Stonehaven and parked in the square, They walked down one of the side alleys that opened out onto the expanse of the stony beach, like a thousand mile journey beneath the unobscured sun and the ghost of a waiting moon between the arms of the cliffs that touched the folds of deep water North and South.

Rachael had said if she could, she'd live in Alford while he might've replied that, had he the choice, he would live in Stonehaven, if only for the beach. He and his sister wandered toward the outgoing tide and watched ragged dogs running along the shore. There was so much space, as if the sea itself was standing off to one side bemused at the arena of the day. And then a darkness fell over him, as if there were no sun, or his sister there beside him, and the gulls overhead were struck dumb by the clamour of the slamming gates in his mind. Then it fell over him and the day was burnt and blackened like some books in a Nazi bonfire fell over him — there was no escape from his head and he would have to go back to the house where he had forgotten how to love.

They must have done some shopping and had a meal. But, before they got back in the car, from some strength of hidden old memories he asked her if they could go to Dunnotar Castle. As if she had been waiting for years for Ash to ask her to take him there, they slammed themselves into the car and she drove swiftly through a thickening of woods beyond Stonehaven and over the sound of falling water like pleasant tinnitus. Finally, along a single track road, they manoeuvred themselves into a tight space in a gravelly car park beside the Exhibition Centre for the castle, at the head of a track that led to the cliffs which overlooked the castle upon its ancient island.

'I haven't been here since mum was still about and even then, I stayed in the car park,' he told his sister. Then with a twinge, like the breaking of a wishbone, he remembered why he had not wandered with her and Mum in her blue raincoat that day, and suddenly he wanted to turn back and hide in the back seat of the sun coloured car. Yet he seemed to have no choice but to walk on to Dunnotar as the upturned steeple of a waterfall drenched down between the vibrant cracks of green hillsides. Often he had gone to the watercolour room in the art gallery just to look at the picture of Dunnotar, standing there, looking closer with such timeless intent as if in the mass of sky, next week's winning lotto numbers were mixed into the paint. Other paler renditions of Dunnotar, dotted about local cafes and in bookshops, in out of the way galleries and his own collection of postcards, but suddenly, as they neared, he finally saw the Dunnotar in its earthly moss and stone.

I could just jump, just run now until I run out of grass and fall into the air, but I can't, and I don't know why I can't. His sister sat upon the edge of the cliff looking down at the communities of seagulls perched upon the cliffside or reeling drunkenly in the happy blue of the sky. She looked down at a line of kayakers, serene, like a family of swans guiding each other along. I could push her off. Now. Now. Or did it seem she was waiting for him to push her off, her back hunched with patient resignation?

He sunk to his knees; the grass was damp but bearable, more bearable than the mass murder in his head as he watched groups of tourists talking snapshots, thinking perhaps, what a great day to have chosen to come here.

How many can I keel over before they get me? He remained rooted to the grass. Oh, don't move. Don't move!

Then he saw her absentmindedly casting him a half smile of recognition. The Rowena he had sat beside at the Rilke night at Books and Beans. Although they had not spoken that night, somehow, he had found her again at the edge of the land, beside his holy castle, this Guinevere that could love him and never ask why.

But Ash hadn't a half bottle of voddie in him to have the balls to go over and say hello. Though it didn't matter in the end, he somehow knew he would see her again when he wouldn't need vodka to speak to her.

His sister got up from the edge, walked over to him, and asked him if had stopped praying yet. He laughed and got up. Before they left, a dad and his weekend son asked them to take a couple of photos, and reciprocated by taking a few of Ash and his sister with Dunnotar in the background. They turned their backs on the castle and too soon they were on the road home to Culter. Ash put his sister's pair of sunglasses on and finally there was a smile in his eyes.

Chapter Twelve

One night, when he couldn't sleep, he lay awake recalling the night in Moorings when he lost his wallet. About the pints of amnesia brew he necked that night, and how he had found himself with a few other men outside the bar after closing hour. The bouncer had popped out for a moment and told them it was time to go home. Ash had found himself walking up Market Street with one of the other stragglers and they kissed and the human world of Saturday strangers closed their eyes to them. They'd kissed three times all the long, beery, cold wind passage up to Rosemount. Ash had fallen into the red, duvet-covered bed and the man lay beside him. Searching through his pockets to make a rolly he discovered he'd lost his wallet. Sobriety in a moment had cleared his head. Thank God, he'd thought. I have to get out of here and the lost wallet panic welled up and he was out, back in the cold windy street.

The nonchalant man still lay upon the bed as Ash had struggled out of the warm, sleep-filled flat to the cold voice of the wind and into a conveniently parked taxi that took him back to his flat. He always had stashed £20 for such an emergency as this. When he had got home, he'd noticed the glass in his watch was broken and the hands clutching onto history. Good watch, he'd thought, best watch I've had. He wondered with a surge of paranoia if the man had tried to stop him leaving and he'd broken his watch on the man in Rosemount's face, but if so, surely he would recall because he hadn't been that drunk. There was no news of a mannie from Rosemount with his head staved in, but Ash did regret breaking the watch. Then there was also the wallet, he'd got all the cards replaced of course but there had been a great picture of Lisa and his sister's dog. Lost. Only a picture, he told himself. This night he lay awake thinking, what if I'd not lost my wallet? Ash played the conversation they'd had in the flat.

"I'm just going to roll up...'

"Then you can suck my cock."

No. There's no way of that happening. Thank fuck I lost my wallet. Ash imagined a scenario where the guy had tried to stop him from going and somehow his good watch was smashed. He tried a few on, but as far as he recalled the guy didn't seem that bothered. Thank fuck I lost my wallet. What if he had tried to stop Ash? It wouldn't have gone well. At the time all he could think of was that he had lost his wallet. He was like a scud missile aimed for home to cancel his cards and ransack the roaches in his ashtray. Thank fuck there was a taxi and he'd got home to a long hangover. A longer week, but as if from a gift of time, that next weekend he had seen Helen for the second time. He'd felt as if he were taking care of a child, he laughed at himself. She was so like me when I was young. He remembered that he had told her that dreaming was pointless. He regretted it, what he'd said. Maybe it was just his dreams that were pointless. Had he given up on everything? Had he stopped dreaming?

Ash got out of bed and he smoked and had a cup of coffee. He checked his phone to see if anyone he knew had called. He usually let the phone ring these days, no one he knew left messages so he didn't know if anyone he knew called. He hated phones. He checked his email. There was a heart-stopper. As he was only in his bare feet, he did not kick the desk in anger. He had not completed his second level creative writing course. He had expected that. If he failed it this time, he would do it another year, he had planned. But, no The OU had banned him from taking courses as he had failed to complete so many. Things were not going the way they were supposed to. Earlier in the year he'd auditioned for a local production of Calendar Girls, but he didn't get the part. Lately he'd been getting more depressed than he realised. He stopped buying newspapers as he couldn't concentrate, as none of it seemed important or relevant to his life now. Yet, he continued. Even if there wasn't a reason.

For months he did not vacuum, only cleaned himself occasionally. Shop for the cats and interminably putting money on his gas or electric card. He'd call his dad, and listen to his sister when she called. The last year or so he'd started seeing a new consultant psychiatrist. She had tried to encourage him with his writing. She also told Ash not to be too hard upon himself. He just didn't know what to do with himself now that he'd finished his first novel. That was the point. He felt he'd been sitting in the same place, drinking coffee and smoking for the last twelve years, and, he told himself forlornly, next year it'll be thirteen.

He stubbed out his last cigarette. As he often did, he told himself that he couldn't put off doing things because today of all days he might write, and he might write something good. How many times had he had the same thoughts, yet still not moved? How many times had he closed the curtains and slept through the day, merely jotting a few things in his journal? The mini-shrink had tried to get him to go to groups. He had nearly cried the last time he saw her. She was pregnant and going on maternity leave. Why did he feel as if he had lost something? Outside the health centre he had to drag himself away from the vicinity of the pub.

Before going back to bed, he looked at the calendar a charity had sent him. In the afternoon he had an appointment with his relatively new psychiatrist. He was quite looking forward to it. He felt she was quite good luck for him. Her name was Helen, like his mum, like the girl from Characters. They had been discussing cutting his meds. He was worrying about the antidepressants. He often ran out of them and his head started to judder, and his tinnitus got really bad. How would he feel if he came off them for good? Would the juddering stop eventually? As he lay there, he tried to remember how he felt before he started those particular pills, but it seemed so long ago. He knew they took an edge off, but he felt he had become less compassionate. And he never had any energy. Back before he took them, he was out walking all the time. Nowadays he felt like a cripple just walking up the hill to his house. Always panting and red-faced when he got back tearing off his clothes as he was so hot.

He lay upon the single bed with an electric lamp on in the far corner. He stared at the books, dusty on a long shelf. Read, read, and not read. He should really give most of them to a charity. Yet some of them were special, even though he wondered if he had been in his right mind when he'd bought some of them. It would be easier to just throw them all in the wheelie bin, he thought, as his sister had told him that charity shops in town weren't accepting books. He looked about the room, cigarette-stained, coffee-coloured, smelling of cat. A looming filing cabinet full of things he'd forgotten about. That can go too; it was ugly and brown like the rest of the room.

In the afternoon he told his psychiatrist about not being allowed to do any more OU courses. She had looked so disappointed in him. He wanted to shout at her, I planned to fail so I could do it another year but they changed the fucking rules on me. The look she gave him said exactly what a failure he'd become, no matter how many people told him not to put himself down, he could not stop the negativity of his thoughts, thoughts that whipped him to his bed and sleep. So he could stop thinking, stop being who he was. They talked about cutting down his medication, but that was all it was. Talking. Giving her a snapshot of my life, as the Eagles used to call it. At least, he thought, as he walked home afterwards, I didn't weep at her. I'm sick of crying. I imagine she is too. Back in the house he made coffee and lit up. I need some help, his thoughts called. I need help to paint the house, vacuum the carpets. He put on a microwave sausage and mash dinner. It tasted like death in his smoke and coffee stained mouth. I need help with everything, he thought as he smoked, staring at the television.

That night, as he always did, he forgot to pray.

Chapter Thirteen

On Thursday, his week's meds gone since last Friday, he was waiting for the long night. But it was only five in the afternoon. No friends were in when he called. Ash had some food — fish fingers and beans with lots of salt. He could hardly bear it with no medication — he felt there was a nuclear bomb testing going on in his brain. He called up his sister again, she could tell he was upset and told him the depression would pass. The next day she surprised him with a visit. She'd brought breakfast. Ash wolfed down the croissant and some fresh pineapple. Ash asked her if she would help him sort his cupboards. Before he knew it, the hall cupboard seemed so spacious there was enough room for a Bulgarian or two, and his wheelie bin was full to bursting with stuff they threw out. He agreed, as there was ample paint to paint the sitting room, to tackle it with her. She was on a mission. The phone went, she was in Lidl and they had good mattresses on offer. Earlier they had inspected his bed; the mattress almost pancake flat and the frame almost bent double. Did Ash want it?

They started the painting early the next day. There was a good calm feeling between them and he did as he was instructed and helped move all the furniture away from the walls. It didn't seem to take that long, he lifted up the red carpet in the hall and white washed it all and the doors. And it wasn't even gone midday. She said she had time if Ash could be bothered to do the bedroom today as well. They got purple paint and got some food, came back and sat in the garden. Ash had a tuna sandwich. Once again, they moved the furniture from the walls and repainted the bedroom purple. She had a grand idea of staining the wooden floorboards. Yet, as if each moment had been spent well, he was surprised to see it was not even five. He suddenly realised he was tired and as she drove away, he closed the curtains and slept on the new mattress on the bed in the middle of the sitting room.

A week or so later the day was fine and he took his camera for a walk over the moor. He was happily snapping away, all worldly concerns vanished as if he were a sphere of light, sure upon the path, that his precious camera created. He fiddled about with it, then, with a howl of despair, fell to the path and started crying like an insomniacal infant. Yet reason snapped him out of it when he saw a woman and dog. Pull yourself together. He saw a sparrow hawk on the pylon, he asked the sparrow hawk to take away the pain. Ash stood up, sniffed, wiped his tears away on his sleeve and walked along the path toward the woman with her dog, to home, to reason.

Two hours later he had come to the resigned consolation that this was karma at work. The last time his friend Martha had visited him, he had inadvertently sat on her camera, he could hear it crunch beneath him and not confessed to it until she was safely back in Edinburgh and on the end of the phone. Now his was fucking, fuck, fucked. Then, he accidentally deleted some pages of a story set in Edinburgh and Glasgow when he went on a site where some of Martha's pictures featured.

Three hours later some witchcraft was involved. He had told his octogenarian neighbours about the night he had sat on her camera and he had them in stitches, yet from then on, he felt a cold whisper reverberating with a harsh future. Did he remember the moment when their curse fell?

After an age it didn't seem to matter how many times he pressed the same buttons on it, the camera was deceased. Why did it seem like the end of the world? He gave up. When he checked in with his sister on the phone, she reminded Ash it was just a possession. Yeah right! As periodically as her periods she would give half her clothes and most of the home furnishings to charity. Ash still had underpants from the last century. What was it with women that they clear out and give away stuff? If it wasn't for her charitable Christian ethic, he would have an extensive library of weird and wonderful books and his well-honed record collection. He said goodbye grumpily. But he wouldn't know what to do without her, she had helped him paint the house and he looked about at how clean and fresh everything was and smiled, and later he bought another a camera from *Amazon*. When it arrived, it needed a memory card so he went to Jessop's, where a tall beautiful woman served him, put in the memory card and the batteries. For the next hour or so he was snapping away about Aberdeen. Some of them were pretty good.

The camera kept him occupied for a week or so when he got into a regime of eating properly and taking the medication as prescribed. Stuck in front of films on the iPlayer. He went down to the shop and met Mark halfway down. Mark told him there was some billy going about. Ash loved speed. He'd not had any for a couple of years. So he wasn't too long behind at Mark's and he got himself some. Sometimes it was so damned convenient with a drug dealer on the other side of the road. But it was good he'd had a break from it — he would enjoy it more now.

He sat in the silent house, the cats sleeping in another room, just listening to his tinnitus. He wrote six chapters of his novel. When the speed ran out, he went back to the boy who was pleased to see him and gave him a couple of lines of cocaine.

That was the way of things before, after and during Christmas. His brother-in-law demanded Ash blow his nose at the Christmas dinner table. He didn't, as he was well aware of the pounds of cocaine compact deep inside his nose. His brother-in-law punished Ash, by putting on opera as they ate the turkey and all the trimmings.

The Wicker Man wasn't on that new year, or *Being There*, He spent the day sleeping as he had done through the royal wedding and the Olympics. Lisa sent him a message to wish him a happy new year, he couldn't reply as he was too hung-over by sleep and boredom. Happy! He thought ruefully. 2013 and all that. Lisa had told him that kids in her school were crying as they were afraid it was the end of the world when the Mayan calendar ran out. Happy! He lay back on the sofa, all the machines off. Well we'd made it through, the Age of Aquarius. At last. Happy. Happy.

Chapter Fourteen

He had the new consultant psychiatrist twice a month now, and a fresh CPN or mental hygienist.

As the Eagles would say, "just a snapshot of your life."

When Ash went to see the consultant, who turned out to be a woman with the same name as Ash's mother. Earlier last year, she said she would cut down his meds as he had been going on about it for months. That was a complete mistake, almost straight away he felt he had lost a leg that he didn't know was there until it was gone. He suffered it for about a month, but had to phone her office to get her to increase his dose of anti-psychotics. It was easier than he thought. He worried too much.

He'd seen the consultant the day his camera broke. There was a kind of hysterical power in the office. Ash told her about all his times in London and how he had found so much more freedom in Glasgow. With each word he could see waves of waxy-like power weeping from him like his tears. He saw her seeing his power sent off to seal the pact through the open window, power slamming into the day. But he was feeling better, he supposed, or so he told her.

Still he was taking all his medication on a Saturday and had to wait a mainly sleepless week until he got more medication. He'd been seeing the consultant about a year and a half when he got his hand on ten jellies. He typed a series of poems in the cold dark of January onto the computer that night. Earlier that day, he asked his dad if he could come out and visit and for once he said he could.

But by then he'd already taken the ten jellies, and he had no meds left to help him sleep. He lay in his bed smoking the tinnitus and bombs going off in his head making him angrier and angrier.

Angry at whom? The usual cavalcade of names and memories attacked Ash with their stock phrases like two dimensional ghosts.

But mainly him. His father. He had stayed up all night making himself sicker, going over the same old arguments so he could not sleep in. And now that it was nearly time to go, the rage within him became so unbearable.

Ash called his dad.

'Right. You! Up!

'You know. I never said this before but the only reason my mum died when she was fifty-nine was because she didn't want to spend any more time with you.' Ash slammed down the phone.

He phoned the octogenarians a couple of doors down the street. 'Look, I'm really sorry for bothering you, but I've been hearing that you go about telling everyone I'm a poor soul. A poor soul...'

'No, we've not been saying that,' they protested.

'All you have to do is apologise and that'll be fine.'

'But that wasn't us.'

'You liar,' Ash screamed down the phone. 'Apologise. Poor soul. Apologise.' He could not stop screaming and slammed the phone down. He snapped in his sister's number and started in on his third phone rage offence of the day, but she was getting slippery and she somehow cut him off.

'What's wrong?'

He howled down the phone, no pain, no words, and a howl that could seem to shatter the world. He hung up and called for an ambulance. He told them that he'd taken fifty jellies. It seemed like only moments before the ambulance men came.

Ash asked the ambulance guy in the back if everyone felt as much pain as this. The guy began to look pale and did not answer. They had to start a conversation as it took at least twenty minutes to get to the hospital and the snow was very thick. His name was Ross. Came from Elgin. Got married and came down here. Ash and Ross were both born in the same hospital. So much for twenty minutes. It took them an hour to get to the hospital, but Ash had someone to talk to.

They wheeled him to the A&E. Inside it was all new and snazzy, not at all busy. He got to lie down straight away and not very much happened as he looked about the department. It was circular in shape with all the beds along the circumference and a nurse's station in the centre. He drank some water. After a while he went to a bed, fell asleep and woke a couple of hours later with drool all down his cheek. He took his jacket with him to the toilet. He lit and took two inhalations of a cigarette.

The next thing he knew he was being discharged and outside by the ashtray for the smokers. He smoked the unfinished cigarette at the entrance, others were also smoking. Then he had a coffee and bacon roll.

He was a bit wobbly, but he was OK. He hardly had to wait for a bus to town, it was busy. He supposed this bus route, that he barely used these days, had a dynamic of its own. He was used to the half empty double decker through Deeside that seemed to wait at each bus stop like some reluctant donkey. (Yeah, the donkey says, I'll help, just let's have a break, please.) While this bus seemed on rails as it sailed on past held up vehicles outside the bus lane. He tried to telephone his sister from a phone box on Union Street — no answer — she was probably at work in the school. The bus for home he saw in the distance turned off Broad Street. He didn't want to hang about town. He easily made it to the bus stop before the bus.

Ash watched the snow fall, as slowly, the surefooted bus took him safely home.

Chapter Fifteen

Ash counted them. Eight. He recognized one of the cops. He could almost feel himself lurch up out of his nest of the long, black leather sofa and go for one of their utility belts. They were waiting for Veronica to drive here from the far side of town.

As soon as he had got home, he had started all over again making abusive phone calls to all and sundry. Someone had called the police. They wanted Vers to stay and look after him. All the while they waited, he ranted about the boy across the road, but he ranted himself into a corner and had to give up his piece of pot.

When she arrived, Ash was hyper, screeching at her as soon as he got in the door, happily like a cat that'd got the cream, giggling, 'I've been busted!'

She insisted on sleeping on the fold down bed under the sofa, but once she'd got it sheeted and cosy with her cuddly toys and the double feather duvet and got in to sleep, it collapsed beneath her. They both laughed. Afterwards, Ash thought if he had just sat and talked with her, in the half light and quietly sitting, instead of chain-smoking, going over everything once again and again, lying in his dirty bedroom all the rest would've been different.

As usual, just after six, he heard the old neighbough, Sarah, take her car out the garage opposite his bedroom window. But, this day, he raced out the back door at her closing the garage door.

'All you have to do is apologise, you fucking witch!' Vers was suddenly at his side pulling him back. Ash struggled from her and raced back into the house grabbed his gnarled, hooked walking stick and began whacking it against their locked front door. Vers was still in the kitchen as Ash broke out into the still dark morn to the front of the houses. The old man, Sarah's eighty-year-old husband, was still in their house. Ash banged and banged his door, screaming 'apologise, that is all I want'. Vers was there again at his shoulder turning him away from the door. Swiftly he ran back into his house, threw down the stick. By the time Vers got back in he'd already picked up the knife. He turned to her and cut twice down his right arm.

'Now have you got what you wanted?' Ash screamed. Blood, yes, but it wasn't spraying all over the place. I've gone too far, he had no choice. Veronica stood for a moment as if she was watching Ash in a play, but when she saw him take a pair of scissors and saw him cut all the wires of his computer all she could weep at him was, 'No'.

Ash felt the electricity like a touch of a snake's tongue, then it was gone and he was still standing.

Then there were more cops. Vers vanished. He was put in an ambulance. Later, in A&E, the nurse chided him for being there a second time as if she were giving him a subtle gift of rational thought. Within minutes they had let him go, and he got lost on the way out. Someone called his name, looking over he saw two cops. For a second, he was terrified, but he went over to them. They'd been at the house earlier, they told him, but he didn't recognise them. However, they were kind and drove him home, via the chemist to get his weeks' worth of pills, and helped him to get the electricity back on. And they called his mental hygienist to make an appointment that day with his psychiatrist. When they left, he slept for the first time that week.

Helen, his doctor, sat in the consulting room, lit sepia brown like an embrace. She liked him. His writing. She was like a bottle of his father's jellies, except he didn't have to steal from her and he didn't have to neck stupid, suicidal amounts of her just to write. Just four or five doses of her a year was ample. He had liked her from the start, even before their first appointment. She had the same name as his mum; Vers had scowled at him when he played at being a sick orphan. 'Where is Dr Helen?' Lisa's middle name was Helen. He'd thought the shrink's last name sounded Scandinavian. When the CPN told him he'd start seeing her, Ash imagined her long, lithe and beautiful, with silver blonde hair. Or he had surmised that she might be married to a Norwegian, then he imagined her on the arm of some wealthy oil worker looking small and weaselly, or maybe he was tall and lanky, and Helen tiny in comparison, with dark hair that fell over her face, small-breasted and so lithe she could float off if she wasn't anchored arm in arm with her warrior of sea and rig, both old and beautiful in a kind of Adam Faith way. Both of them dressed in clothes that seemed like a creative skin from the souls of people living in a land of winter. When Ash imagined them apart, her man was diminished without her and he had the look of a lost child in big city while she would dance on the frosty air. Her eyes would be as dark as her hair and if she smiled at you they would glint star light, black like the long nights of the North. And then when she spoke it was like a surprise, strangers would expect that she spoke French for she seemed like an aristocrat exiled, strangers might expect her to speak Mandarin, for she was graced with a deceptive fragility. Ash would voice the words that her tongue-tied husband had neither the wit nor imagination to say; Ash would tell no earthly language should touch that heart red tongue and lips, but only the words of an angel or an alien. Yes, if Ash could put these words into the clumsy roustabout spouse's mouth, she would smile and laugh lovingly at his praise, laughter like a miracle giving sight to those lifelong blind, and a smile like a blessing from a prophet.

But at their first meeting she turned out to be a middle-aged, non-blonde, small English woman. He was really disappointed her name was Helen and that was the point. There was something magical about her anyway. Nevertheless, she seemed to dust all the long neglected bookshelves in him by the time he'd left the consulting room after that first appointment and only a few days later he had met that other Helen in Characters. His Dr Helen seemed to grant his secret wish, unspoken, but long, long desired.

Now, a year later in the twilit, almost sleeping consulting room, she let him tell the tale of the worst day of his life and she did not allow him to see how tired she was. She offered him a bed at the hospital if he wanted to be admitted as a voluntary patient, she seemed to be offering to even drive him there. Stubbornness and the last few roaches in his roach bags, stopped him from going with her and he dragged himself back home, yet she had left the place open if he changed his mind.

Yet once he got home he felt like a terrified ghost haunted by the living. For a moment or two as he sat on the red carpeted floor, he was glad he had once again avoided the Bin that came with the memories of months in Kingseat, month long sections, and fortnightly injections, freedoms curtailed. He'd avoided the primal fear of that hospital which came from a similar place as ancestral fears of slavery. Yes, glad for a moment until he realized how cold with loneliness his house was, and silent, a sad sitting room with its many empty chairs, his own self-enforced lifetime section filled with angry conversations with the ghostly patients in his mind.

Once he rolled up a roach filled full, of dry tobacco and old ash, Dr Helen's kind words, as if from somewhere long, long ago, returned to him with each harsh drag of the number. The joint lasted a long time, the smoke like a faded suit wreathed and swam about him. He felt he had been dumped suddenly into the future where all the rules of his life had been ripped up and he did not know what to do.

He called Dad. Max 2 barked in the background. Dad begged Ash almost in tears to take the place at the hospital and within an hour he had entered the TV room of a ground floor ward.

Part 2

Chapter One

Charlotte asked him how to use the remote control.

'I've no idea. I just got admitted.'

'Oh.' Charlotte looked almost in tears. Ash thought her whole body seemed to be weeping, her hair drenched in tears from a lifetime of blubbering.

'Let me have a go, then.'

She smiled like a dream of sunrise, like a surprise of sunshine evaporating the lingering dew in him.

'So why are you in?'

He revealed the knife slashes down his arm.

'Have you been sectioned?'

'No. I'm voluntary. My dad was almost crying on the phone, he begged me to come in. He shamed me in the front door.'

'Is the ward door locked?' Ash nodded. 'Oh. I'd have to speak to one of the nurses now.'

Charlotte walked away towards the nurses' station leaving Ash in frustration with the battery-less remote. Then he saw the manual controls on the side of the TV and gently manipulated them until he finally got a picture as Charlotte knocked loudly on the door of the nurses' station. Ash channel surfed and sat tiredly, his fingers numb, and laughed for the first time in days when he found an episode of *The Big bang Theory* on E4. Charlotte returned and sat beside him.

'Do you like this?' he asked.

'Can you get Al Jazeera?' she responded.

'OK.' He got up again a stabbed at the controls at the side of the TV.

'No, you've got to go back up. Those music channels have been on since I got sectioned.'

Ash sighed wearily, then the video of Annie Lennox's *No more I love yous* distracted him from his utter exhaustion and he asked her, 'Can I watch this first?'

'Are you sectioned?' she repeated. 'Do you want to go for a fag?' She offered him a Regal.

'Thanks. I suppose we have to go outside?'

'Yeah. There's a garden.' She pointed to a doorway wedged open with books. He followed after her, his Regal stuck unlit between his lips like a rude, sickly tongue and, once through the door he sparked up his old lighter that Helen had given him, and lit hers first.

Snow covered the garden ahead of them and more was falling, a wind blasted at them and the others crowded outside the doorway all blowing their smoke as if their silver blue breaths could battle the waves of wind.

Chapter Two

'I just thought,' Ash said to Charlotte as the automatic doors of the bank slid open. 'Perhaps back on George Street there was some time-travelling anthropologist come from the far future to study us as we are the forebears of a genetic pool that has great significance in their time.'

She said, 'Even I know that's a bit far-fetched.'

'Anything's possible.'

Charlotte had joined the end of the queue. Two customers were being served and ahead of Charlotte in the line were a diminutive, soft bodied, thin and blonde woman Ash thought he recognized from somewhere, and she was telling the nervous man ahead of her that the cash machine wasn't working and it was her son's birthday. Charlotte anxiously watched a well-dressed, looming tall black-skinned teller with teeth whiter than his well ironed shirt as he served a large sweaty man in dirty grey tracksuit bottoms with a matching dirty grey sweatshirt. The slob was telling the teller how he had tried to use the cash machine. He seemed drunk and was listing all the things he had planned to buy with his money. Even though there was a rising urgency in his voice, there seemed a precise confidence in it that held a bank robber's gun to the black man's head, and each knowing, well-placed word was like a wish or a prayer or a magic spell that would, without doubt, give him power to unlock the cash he wanted. Along from him at the counter a couple stood. They looked like tourists or immigrants, young, holding each other; they seemed to Ash as vulnerable as young kids playing Mary and Joseph in a nativity play in front of the whole school. Their teller stared at the bank details on her computer screen as if she was telepathically trying to fit together whatever was awry with the couple's account. She excused herself and went through a door behind at the back of the counter where a greater mind than hers could be found; perhaps the Wizard of Oz. Mary asked her Joseph in their own language what was happening, but Ash saw how his slumped shoulders emphasised his hopelessness, as if he were too tired to explain. The teller returned, a *no, we can't help you,* on her face. Broken, almost in tears, Mary turned from the counter and Ash watched them sorrowfully leave the fully booked Bethlehem Inn through the bank's automatic doors and disappear down Hadden Street, still holding each other as if that were the only currency they had left. Meanwhile the slob had become silent as if he'd so befuddled the black teller that he was counting out cash just to shut up the grey-garbed guy. The small woman ahead of Charlotte was speaking into a mobile phone. Charlotte was looking worried with waiting. Ash attempted a smile for her. He liked the open-plan, almost friendly environs of the bank. In the centre of it were two soft cushioned settees facing each other. He told Charlotte he was going to sit down. She shushed him, as her eyes bored into the black teller like she were telepathically urging him to get his finger out and serve her first instead of the woman speaking on her phone. Ash moved away and thankfully dropped onto one of the sofas facing the automatic doors, wishing desperately that he could run out, away from Charlotte, as fast as he could.

The doors slid open and his friend Alison entered the bank. He thought she looked thinner, all dressed up and looking the best he'd seen her. A younger woman came in at the same time and Ash assumed this was Alison's daughter. He called Alison over and she sat beside him.

'Is that Lea?'

'No, nothing to do with me. What are you doing here?' Ash points at Charlotte.

'Have you known her for a while, or did you just pick her up?' Alison asked.

'We met in the hospital.' And he showed her the cuts on his arm.

'Oh.' She was quiet for a moment or two. 'I have a new number if you want it.' He scribbled it down on the back of a bank withdrawal slip. Alison got up and told him to take care and went to use the cash machine for deposits at the back of the bank.

Looking back over at Charlotte he saw her eyes looking at Alison and switching to him with a look full of poison and hopeless failure. She beckoned for him to come over to the queue which somehow hadn't moved forward. Both tellers had vanished from the counter and the woman with the phone was almost shouting at the black plastic in her hand as if it were a very naughty boy. As he returned to Charlotte's side, he could see she was in tears.

Oh fuck, he thought. 'What's up, sweetie?'

'I need my money now.' She snapped as if he were responsible for the wait and that he had stolen the purse she had lost in hospital.

He gave her shoulders a squeeze. She tried to smile through a hiccup of tears, but there was a terrible strength in her voice as she said, 'I want it now.' Ash cringed and felt all the eyes in the bank fall on him. Then, desperately attempting to calm her and stop the crying, he spoke the magic words that had stilled her weeping in the past.

'I'll scream and scream until I'm sick.' He smiled, put his hand beneath her chin and lifted her head so their eyes met and saw she was suddenly smiling at his fake mockery. 'Because I can.' He tickled her under the chin and she laughed, and it seemed the bank full of folk sighed with relief. Charlotte put her arm through his. Finally the white-teethed, beautiful bank teller beckoned her over and Ash, relieved, almost fell back into the sofa. He heard her blubbering out her story about the stolen purse while the teller nodded benignly as if he had heard her telling the same story in a dream he'd had the night before. And about all the cards on a day trip one horrible day away from the ward. Ash drifted off thinking about Alison, he memorised her new number and put it into the back of his wallet like valuable keepsake of his holiday in the bank on Hadden Street. As if the black guy was either stupid or deaf, Charlotte repeated the same story Ash had heard many times, thinking what he would do once the torture of the day in the uncomfortable energy of Charlotte was over and he could go home to skin up the last of his legal highs. That is if the day would ever end, he still had to get Charlotte back to the hospital. Please give her some fucking money. He looked over at the counter and the black teller had moved away to speak with someone who might be, please Jove let it be, the bank manager.

Charlotte walked serenely over to him, so calm now after all the scenes and almost hysteria, as if she were a completely new person he had never met before, a stranger who was incapable of weeping, her face covered in a make-up of joyfulness that forbade tears.

'Who were you talking to before?'

'Just a pal I haven't seen for a while.'

'I don't like her.'

'So are they giving you anything?'

'Maybe a hundred. I have to speak to an advisor.'

'Great. That should last you.'

She sat close beside him and kissed him with salty lips. Soon a couple of the bank staff came over to them on the sofa and asked Charlotte to join them in a partitioned off part of the bank. Ash said he would wait where he was but the two advisors implored him with their eyes to come with him should the necessity of his magic over Charlotte be required. Inwardly he groaned. This has nothing to do with him. Did they think he was her CPN, or social worker? He wanted to run away as fast as he could, but Charlotte took his hand and almost dragged him after the two advisors and he found himself sitting beside her facing the two bank staff is if it were him facing the guillotine and not Charlotte.

'Well,' she said rudely, 'Are you going to give me some cash?'

Yeah, that's the way to go, sweetie, that's going to get them to give you the key to the safe. He squeezed her hand so hard his nails almost cut into the palm of her sweaty hand. He looked in disbelief as one of them got her to sign a withdrawal slip and the other counted out five £20 notes.

'There, are you OK now?' he asked. But, no…

She let go his hand and snatched up the money and put it in her purse that looked suspiciously like the one she had supposedly lost and asked if she'd be able to get more until she got her new card. Ash almost cried out. Isn't that enough, don't push it. One of the advisors looked at Ash and shook her head as if it were all his fault that Charlotte couldn't get any more money, that it was him that had spent it all, stolen the purse and was using Charlotte for booze money.

Help, this has nothing to do with me, it's her that gives fivers away to every homeless gypsy she crosses, her that spends twenty quid on fags that lasts her half an hour. Her. He wanted to bang his head on the table between them. They looked at the computer as if it showed an aid worker being beheaded by terrorists.

'Well, your account is quite overdrawn. So, I'm sorry, this is the last money we can give you until new funds go into it.'

Charlotte straightened up and looked at them icily and said, 'Well I suppose I'll just have to wait until my dad dies, eh?'

Ash took her shoulders and gently turned her to him. 'Hey.' He smiled somehow. 'Why don't we just go back up the road so you can get your supper?

'OK then.' She smiled at him and a little of the embarrassing dread he felt dissipated. The two advisors smiled at him, appreciating his messianic power over her. He took her hand and urged her from the seat and she stood and looked about the bank as if in shock. She clutched the purse in her other hand, precious as the touch of an only son. He led her from the bank. As soon as the automatic doors of the bank shut behind them Charlotte went into shop-shop-shopping mode and, to Ash's surprise, had spent the whole hundred quid by the time they got to the rain-drenched, wind-whipped hospital. By then, Ash thought he would fall over and considered admitting himself back into the hospital, any ward where Charlotte wasn't. At the door of the ward, she grabbed the bags of charity shop clothes and the £50 of groceries she'd bought for all the Chancers within. Ash was relieved she left him there; he escaped to a smoking shelter and vainly hoped he would never see her again.

Chapter Three

After Ash had made Charlotte come and she tried to snuggle into bed beside him he pushed her away without screaming at her to leave him alone, without screaming why are you here all the time, without screaming at her vile face, her ugliness, her obscene body: get out. Get away from me! Instead, he said calmly, as if he knew it was the best way to cut her to the bone, as if he knew such a calm voice would convey the bitterness and vile poison in him, 'Would you write me a reference? I'm looking for a younger model.' Then, after her silence, he added, 'Could you leave me to sleep?' She straightened her clothes and went through to the sitting room, calling back. 'What do you want me to do?'

'God's sake, Charlotte, put on the radio, read a bloody book, paint something.'

For half an hour Ash tried to sleep almost forgetting she was still in the house. Then he heard the front door opening. 'At last.' But she did not slam the door behind herself and a few seconds later came back in and he was overwhelmed by the sickening thought that she would never go. The cops would come again to take her back to the hospital and he'd have to ignore her innumerable phone calls that would spoil another day filled with the dread that she would turn up once more in a taxi. And it would start all over again and she would let him make her come again, and he'd have to repress the spew of all the filth and black thoughts she provoked in him. Would he ever sleep now she was a constant presence in his life? How many pillows with her face imagined on it would he have to batter? Go away. Go away, Please, God, if I see her fucking face, I'll puke.

Then he heard the distinctive knock of the guy from over the road, the dealer, Mark, on the door and swiftly Charlotte opening the door. He heard the junkie's voice.

'Did you put this in my letterbox?' She said yes and closed the door as Mark went away.

Ash's anger coursed through his livid body. Him. Him. She'd brought that cunting pusher to his door. What is wrong with her? He threw back the bedclothes and, half dressed, raced through to the sitting room. As calmly as he could he told Charlotte, 'Please will you just leave — please?'

'OK,' she said. He sat in his shirt and underpants on the long, black couch as she slowly wandered about picking up and bagging up her stuff. She piled her bags by the door. Surely it couldn't be that easy. He smiled inwardly, works every time, saying please. Charlotte came into the sitting room, but just stood by the end of the sofa.

'Could you lend me a tenner?'

Ash thought of the line from *Dr Zhivago*:

'I have paid my whore; I give her to you as a wedding gift.'

And the line raged and repeated behind his false, cruel, empty-eyed face as he ripped open his wallet and gave her cash. Charlotte smiled her thin-lipped smile, almost triumphant. And she thanked him as if he were not throwing her out, but she abandoning him, never to please him again, never to make her come again. A smile that showed Ash she had beaten him and his greedy, mean-minded genes. With the smile left on the air in front of him, she went from the end of the couch to the kitchen. He groaned and lit up, thinking, I'll have to go out to get another pack of twenty. He heard her in the kitchen running water in the washing-up bowl.

What is she doing now?

'Please,' he repeated, 'Charlotte, will you go.'

She stamped through the hallway; picked up her bags and the door shut quietly like the whispering voice of his Grandfather's last words. She was gone, and Ash was glad. Suddenly, the house was silent and he felt emancipated to sleep for as long as he liked, or to talk to himself and do whatever he fucking felt like doing, for the next three years. But, instead, for the next three years she was always there, in his head, the pictures and the scissors she had left behind, following him when he went out, at every rage filled corner on the periphery of the day. All the hate for her he did not express, all the cruel jibes he had stifled, ate at him, broke him. He felt all her otherworldly orgasms and as he struck each new pillow, wondered if she would ever leave him alone, in the peace of sleep, in the freedom of dreams where she did not venture, on his murdered misshaped pillows. And like the wedded couple she desired them to be, each day free of Charlotte was devoid of marital bliss and the crying of their aborted, unmade babies, imprisoned in masturbatory separate bedrooms, crusty with the orgasms of waste. He felt like a widower, released from the responsibilities he had run away from when he asked her that sunny day in spring three years ago today to please go away. Please. Charlotte haunted Ash and the younger model he never found.

Chapter Four

The latest mental hygienist, Linda, was late, or Ash was far too early. The waiting room was packed and too hot so he went back out again and leant against the wall of the health centre with a view of the car park. He didn't know what Linda's car looked like so he scrutinised each car passing or coming into the car park, dismissing them all. He lit up using Helen's lighter and his eyes were drawn to the gay guy across the road hitting on a couple of plumbers by their van. So he missed Linda parking her car and she came upon him unawares. He dropped the butt and stuttered, 'It's too hot in there, had to get some fresh air.' He followed her in through the sliding doors, she went into the reception area to get his notes and for a minute or two he perched on the only available seat, anxious and self-conscious as if the whole of the village had turned up just to see him suffering in the damnable heat. Thankfully Linda wasn't long and they went, like a swiftly cruising bus down the bus lane ahead of a traffic jam at the Handigain Roundabout, into the Community Consulting Room. In the same way he had disliked his mini-shrink, he liked the mental hygienist. The fact that Linda was small and blonde while the mini-shrink was dark and big was a major factor, yet Linda was part of Dr Straven's team, while the mini-shrink was part of The Eagle's team, his last psychiatrist whom he'd sacked for putting him on the evil Valium and demonic anti-depressants. Also, while he had missed countless appointments with the mini-shrink, Ash had religiously turned up each time to see Linda. However, he couldn't look Linda in the eye, or sometimes even look at her at all. She saw him looking intently at electric sockets, or seemingly redesigning the carpet with his mental powers, or fiddling about with stuff on the desk, but not ever Ash's eyes.

He had been out of the ward about a month so he showed her the photos he'd taken on the camera Veronica had given him as he'd wandered about the village and down by the River Dee. He admitted, that apart from doing that, he'd done no writing and had been having a vast number of vivid dreams.

'Once or twice I've been in town. First time I went to that drugs action place,' he scowled. 'You know that place on Market Street. Dr Straven said I'd get help there. But, I must have gone on the wrong day or the wrong time or I didn't look wasted enough to get help so there was no room at the inn so to speak. So that was the day... he paused.

'Do you want to know a secret?' She nodded. 'I came out the DA place and crossed Market Street, as if the hand of fate was on my shoulder, into the market, straight to the legal high shop.'

Linda sighed as if she'd heard it all before.

'Well don't you think that's a bit unwise?'

'Probably, but it's better than the hassle of getting illegal highs and having to associate with my junkie friends.'

She said nothing for a while, so he asked her if he could stand and walk about a bit. Linda told him she didn't mind.

He lumbered up to his feet, but felt stupid in the cramped little room as if he was doing a crazy and felt as if Charlotte had taken over his body, so he sat straight back down again.

'So how are you managing with the daily dispense?'

'That's about the only good thing. I get out every day, do photos and that because I have to go the chemist. I love walking down by the river and my legs are thick with muscles. So yes, it's OK.'

Thankfully the hour-long appointment sped by and, unlike the mini-shrink, the mental hygienist never asked the final, dreaded question, 'Is there anything else I can help you with?'

If Linda had, he would've asked her for a lift into town, but anyway he was free to frogmarch out of the place and almost ran to the bus stop. Just as well, as the bus arrived in less than a minute to take him into town. He flashed his concession card and stamped up the stairs to the top deck. For once the bus was fleet-footed and hardly missed a green light or stopped to pick up any other travellers. He threw the crappy free newspaper off the seat. Might as well read *The Sun*. He later realised he could have used it to line the cat litter tray, but that rag wasn't even worthy of that. He stared out the window, watching the horses in the fields just outside Culter and the start of major road works preparing the way for the new fabled Aberdeen Bypass. Swiftly, they reached Milltimber Church, the empty cross draped with a white sheet as it would soon be Easter, then they were in Cults where a new old folks' home had just opened. Then, just a mile or two from the city centre, the bus came to a rude halt at the crossroads just after Mannofield and the bus took three or four attempts to get by the traffic lights. After that they were home free and he considered where to get off the bus, playing with the pack of eighteen and Helen's lighter in his coat pocket.

He got off by the graveyard and quickly crossed the vehicle-less void of Union Street and into the side entrance to the Market. He got himself a three gram bag of Clockwork Orange and a gram of Croackcaine, plus his usual £1 worth of cheap ciggie papers that the older woman behind counter threw in, when she served him. Then, just as quickly, he retraced his steps out of the Market to the bus shelter just outside the entrance. A bus came just as he was thinking of buying a book to read on the way back so he spent another illiterate journey back to Culter.

If Ash had known then that he would be repeating the same journey to the legal high shop, apart from varying the time spent in the city centre in Waterstones or cafes and charity shops, picking up food and falling in love with a girl in the Co-op and another in Poundland, for the next two and a half years, no doubt he would've regretted the cunning plan he had made. The plan being that he would wean himself off proper drugs and avoid the associated trouble with drug dealers, especially the boy, Mark, the junkie over the road and, all in all, cut down smoking in all forms. But Ash being Ash, he should've known none of his cunning plans would come to fruition.

Chapter Five

Ash was in town, moving swiftly through daily routine and perfect round. He stood at the steps of the Market, he had come to a stop. He didn't know his next move, whether to go up to a coffee shop or down to the harbour. He turned down the cobbled street to avoid a hard-faced, desperate prostitute. Ash found himself at the back of Moorings and decided to go in, it had been over two years since he'd last had a drink and, who knows, he might see Helen in there.

He ordered a pint and checked out the small group of goths, the woman by the window reading a newspaper, on the juke box Siousxie and the Banshees was playing, but halfway through some kind of German rock bands started up.

He ordered a beer and told the barman that he thought German voices and singers a special sort; he told the barman that a song in *Cabaret*, *Tomorrow Belongs to Me*, was beautiful. Then he thought, he probably thinks I'm a lover of musical theatre.

Halfway through the second pint he realised that the lone woman with a paper was a prostitute and ordered a packet of cigarette papers. He went swiftly to the toilet to skin up some legal highs, but it stank of barman's shit and there was nowhere to lean his makings on, even the floor was all pissy so he decided not to bother, went out and, after the last half-pint, he got himself out of the pub.

Ash went to look for somewhere quiet to skin up. Despite the wind and the occasional person passing by, he managed in twice the time it usually took, to build a half-decent, smokable spliff. He sat and looked out at the boats anchored at the wharf side, vast supply boats and, over in the distance, the ferry to Shetland where Charlotte lived. But suddenly a tough wind smacked into him as he stared and grit brought tears to his eyes. Ash decided to go home now, so he turned his back on the harbour, walked up Market Street and along Union Street to the Co-op. He saw Rob the Artist at the self-service checkout, buying a couple of beers.

'Rob,' Ash shouted excitedly. He waved over and they met at the entrance and walked down to Union Terrace Gardens so Bob could drink his beers. Ash took out the gram of Charlie Sheen, wet his finger and had a few dabs. Bob offered him a beer, not noticing what Ash had done. Ash asked for a cigarette as he'd forgotten to get any in the Co-op. Rob said he was out and proffered the open can. But Ash was lost without a fag to skin up, looking about for dog ends in the grass. He saw a lassie over on one of the green benches and started to approach her. She was eating a sandwich.

'Hello.' He was met with silence. 'I don't suppose…'

'No!'

He retreated back to Rob in the grass, and asked him if he'd been doing any painting.

'No, but I've been doing a lot of drinking.' And offered the beer once more.

'Do you want to look at some photos? I got a new digital camera.' Ash tried to show him his latest batch of pictures of the reconstruction of Marschall College into the new Council Headquarters, but the evening light came stuttering through the trees that encircle the gardens and made it difficult to see the pictures.

Ash was a bit disappointed and Rob looked cross when Ash grabbed the camera away from him and put it in his pocket. He took another dab of Charlie Sheen.

'I wish you could read my novel.'

Bob asked, 'Is it all typed?'

'Yes.'

'Well give me a look, if you still want me to.'

'Let's go up to Union Street. I fancy a drink,' Ash decided

'I know a place where there's a beer garden.'

Ash felt the pints from Moorings kicking in as they sat in the rather tiny beer garden sandwiched between the TSB and the dentists. They were talking about a mutual friend Ash hadn't seen for years. He lived in an estate up by the hospital.

'I'll give you his new number as long as you don't tell him I gave it to you,' Rob offered.

Ash wrote it down in the blue spiral notebook he'd bought in the post office when he applied for his passport, between an unfinished poem and pages of a hangman game he'd played one night with Charlotte.

Once they'd drunk up, Rob said he was going to the Holburn Bar so Ash traipsed along and got some cash from the hole in the wall on the corner of Union Street. He gave Bob £20, saying, 'You need it more than me and, anyway, if I'm in dire straits one day, maybe someone'll do the same for me.'

Rob nodded sagely.

At the Holburn, downstairs wasn't open yet so they went into the bar. Between sips of a vodka and coke, Ash dabbed at the Charlie Sheen in his pocket. Somehow the desolate bar had become a party and he found himself dancing with an obese woman he'd spoken to when they came in.

A guy on Facebook looked pissed off at them and slammed down the lid of his massive laptop and left. Ash went out for a cigarette and the postie who had been sitting at the end of the bar was at the door, smoking out of the wind. Ash couldn't stop himself from thanking the postal service and all who sailed in her for the great service they had done to his writing career. He would've hugged the postie but he could tell the guy was gay so didn't bother.

Soon the club downstairs was open and Ash and Rob went down. He gave Rob a tenner to get a round then went to the toilet to skin up, but he was a bit jittery and dropped the joint into the toilet bowl. Waste not want not, he told himself, and fished it out and carried the slimy wet worm of legal highs through to the club that was filling up with folk and a band was playing. The joint felt and looked unsmokable in the buzz and half-light, so he cast it aside onto the floor.

Meanwhile Rob still hadn't got the beers. A barman called him over, as Rob had pointed at him.

'Yes, I gave him the money,' Ash replied.

When the bar tender asked how much he'd given Rob, Rob had told a porky and said Ash had given him twenty. He answered, 'Oh, just a tenner.' He wasn't in the least aware of Rob's duplicity. Rob's look growled at Ash and dejectedly Rob took the change. Ash went to find a place to watch the band; the noise was far too loud so he retreated back to where Rob was sitting with their drinks. They sat in silence for a while; Ash gawped about the place as more and more folk came in.

'I think I'll stay in here for now,' Ash said.

Bob had drunk his pint and was looking uncomfortable. Nearby, two lassies had set up a couple of tables to flog CDs of the night's band, so when Rob pissed off, Ash went over to them feeling daft with cash and bought one. He suddenly wanted to go after Rob and give him some more money so he could feed himself. He found him in a doorway across the road. Ash sat beside him.

'God, I'm away with it!' His dabbing finger searched for the powder at the bottom of the gram bag.

Is it OK to skin up here? He went ahead anyway but the skins wouldn't stick together and the wind kept pushing them away and spread the contents everywhere. He gave up.

'Here's some money to buy food.' Rob took it.

'You know you're the only friend I have left. Do you remember when you came to live at my bit, and then left the next morning, because I told you to paint a picture of the stars?

Rob grinned.

'I'm going to Edinburgh for the festival. Do you want to come with me? You can make a mint begging down there...

'Yeah, I can imagine. I like the buskers, music on every corner.'

'What are you going to do now?' Rob asked.

'I'm going back into the Holburn, and then maybe go down the Lane'.

'It's not safe down there. Be careful.'

Ash went back over the road. As he ordered he told the barman he'd given Rob £20 to get some scran

'£20', the barman laughed. 'It's you that...'

But Ash turned his back on him and went and watched the second band of the night. He saw some free seats on the front so went down the aisle of merrymakers. He was happy on the front with a great view of the band. In very little time he found himself lying down alone along the empty seats. He saw one of the lassies who'd been flogging the CDs giving him a look. He lurched over to her.

'Don't you think you've had too much to drink?'

She was probably right. 'OK, I'll have one more and go.'

She came over to the bar with Ash and watched him drink down the lager. By the end of the first half-pint everything that followed was taken from his mind, blanked out until he found himself getting out of a taxi in front of his house. And, for no reason he could recall, he was at the back of Mark and Juliet's house screaming and shouting abuse after bashing his face on the tall fence at the side of their garden. He felt a cut and there was blood on his fingers and his glasses were left askew halfway down his nose. Then, until the policeman came he repeatedly shouted "Die", at Mark's window, and "Fucking Junkies", and "Juliet, yeah you, die you Junkie bitch", over and over mixing all three until his lungs were heaving with the effort.

The policeman found him lying by the steps to his back door still screaming at Mark and Juliet, who hadn't come out of their house, even though Ash could hear them stopping each other from doing him in. With just a few looks and words the policeman had snapped him out of his psychotic glee. The tall, good-looking copper took Ash's keys and helped him inside. In the kitchen, in the blaze of light, Ash started up again screaming more tasteless abuse, especially directed at Juliet. The policeman spoke on his radio and within a few minutes a young lassie cop arrived in the kitchen, but still he couldn't stop shouting, shouldn't stop screaming. The tall, good-looking policeman with surprising strength, which Ash couldn't have resisted, even if he'd tried, had him handcuffed and lying face down in the cat's food bowl.

'That's it,' he said. 'You're arrested.'

'Aberdonian fuck…' And then the bile and hatred, the sheer evil he had had to contend with from his first days in Aberdeen, in school, and all the other days of his time in this place was rammed out of him like tainted blood and plueretic snot. The door was still open and a stream of new cops came into the kitchen. He screamed out louder, his voice directed now at all the neighbours' houses. The mean-minded street full of thoughtless, uncaring servants of his ire, those most of all responsible for the hatred he felt, the sheer rage of fifty years directed solely at them. He needed most of all to let them know how much he despised them. 'Ya, Aberdonian assholes.' His arresting officer pushed his face deeper into the cat's food and, as he twisted about his head, tried to gag him with a tea towel to shut him up.

Ash told him that he needed to go the toilet. 'Well you should have thought of that earlier. You're not going anywhere now.'

Ash was taken out of the kitchen by the three cops who'd been the last to witness his anti-social behaviour;

they threw him into the back of the police van. Ash realised it was something they did every day, and as he was driven away, felt there was no malice in them towards him, it was almost an act of kindness. A small dribble of urine escaped, but he tensed up to stop the inevitable flow from being released.

In no time Ash was at the police station, just behind the Arts Centre where he'd once been in a one man show, still in the excruciatingly tight handcuffs. He was taken to the front desk by the first two cops.

The tall one wanted to hit him, Ash could tell, the tall one wanted to kill him. Just like a fucking Aberdonian, he thought.

Luckily, before he let the bladder full of lager tasting urine escape all over himself and the police station floor, the lassie copper searched him and found his legal highs.

'I don't drink very much,' Ash said apologetically.

She was going to search him for illegal highs but he shook his head to save her the bother and then proceeded to piss himself.

In the cell he took off his clothes and they put them in a bin bag and they gave him a pair of plastic pyjamas. After they closed his cell, he realised it was the cell they had always put him in.

'I was better,' he cried out at the empty walls and unopenable door. 'I was better.' He could hear others in their adjoining cells shouting and screaming and he could hear his own voice in theirs so he shut up howling at the wind and suddenly stopped being so angry. Later the grille on the cell door opened and one of the women at the front desk told him that Veronica was coming to pick him up. In ten minutes or so the tall cop came to the grille and showed him his arrest docket. Ash raised himself up from the lotus position and agilely went to look at it. The copper pointed out the website he would have to use to pay his fine and Ash had to push his face further into the open grille to scrutinise it, squinting as they had taken his glasses. Then suddenly the lassie cop was at the other's shoulder. Ash felt the anger emanating from the guy and pushed his head back out of the grille, sure that his much abused, helplessly angered, arresting officer was going to smash Ash's head into the top of the grille.

Ash thought I wouldn't blame him, he could have had that one for free and I wouldn't complain.

They gave him his clothes and his legal highs, but he had no wallet and he recalled that his glasses got broken when he bumped into the fence beside Mark and Juliet's bit. A portly cop he remembered from another night in the cells, took him to the reception where Veronica was waiting. He said, 'Don't give her a hard time.'

Ash playfully punched the master of the keys in the stomach. 'Yeah, I'll be good. See Ya.'

And then he rushed over to his beautiful sister and told her, 'Oh, it's so good to see you.'

Chapter Six

Ash had been on daily dispense since he'd been discharged from hospital. Basically daily dispense meant that he had to go down to the village chemist every day except Sundays to collect his medication. He'd been doing so for nearly a year now. Once he'd tried to go back on weekly dispense but he'd taken all his pills in a couple of days and within the week he was back on daily dispense. He told Sandra, the chief chemist, that he felt Dr Straven had been bullying him to get his meds weekly.

'Don't let her bully you,' Sandra had said. He'd nearly been in tears at his failure, but there were more pros than cons getting daily dispense. He went out more, going into town for his legal highs, food, buying books, but mainly getting out of Culter where the prices of most things were ridiculously high. He was getting fitter, going up and down the hill every day, walking along the riverbank or over the road to the moor, or marching from one charity shop, or coffee shop, to the next along Union Street. He took more showers and shaved every day, even got into a house cleaning routine, and he ate far better than he had for years.

Yet every time he saw his psychiatrist he felt she wasn't listening to him when he told her how much better his life had become. Once, while he was waiting for his next appointment, Ash thought, I dare her, just one fucking word about my pills and I'll walk out.

But, of course, this time she never said a word and, until she quit a few months later, going off daily dispense wasn't mentioned again. However, then she started on at him about seeing a psychotherapist, but he dug in his heels, he was fine with her and his mental hygienist and didn't want a change. One month she might say he wasn't getting much from his visits with her, or the following month he might say he had been killing time until the appointment by cleaning his house and she said he might as well have just kept on cleaning instead of wasting time with her.

Didn't she realise that he felt so at ease with her, felt she was the only shrink he had properly spoke with in all his years of shrinking? She was driving him away into the arms of some analyst he was beginning to fear each time she mentioned him, so when one month she asked him straight out if he wanted to be put on the waiting list for a psychotherapist he politely refused. Ash didn't want anything else, she was his lucky charm and there every month for him to blether at. But with every word, sigh, incline of her head, she deflated him, trying to drive him away.

Then one day, almost two years since being discharged from the hospital, Dr Straven almost broke him, seemed to want to send to him to the pub at the bottom of the hill as soon as he left the health centre, or leave him weeping out in the street.

'Well, Ash, I have to give up my position at the hospital as my mother is very sick and I have to spend time taking care of her.'

Ash was surprised and the thought 'another one bites the dust' sprang into his mind, but it wasn't funny. His stomach wanted to empty on the swivel chair at the side of the desk and such an awful pain stabbed into his smoky soul. From outside he could hear the mocking laugh, laugh, laughing of children. He stood; there would be no ritual of filling out the appointment card, Dr Straven going through her diary to give him a look at all the things she had to do. He made it to the door of the office struggling to put his coat on. She seemed to be saying something but he couldn't hear her over the shrill of whistling tinnitus. He stared at the grain of the office door. Ash said, 'Well, bye, I'll see you, no I won't but you know what I mean.' He finally managed to get into his coat and opened the heavy door leaving her behind, a piece of his dead past, and walked out without looking back.

Chapter Seven

Ash's mental hygienist, Linda, gave him more of a forewarning of his banishment. She painstakingly explained to him about his illness — which wasn't at all what he thought it was — the causes and its symptoms. As he walked home from the health centre just before Christmas, he had a kind of revelation, a presentiment of the future as the understanding lay before him like the footprints ahead that he would leave in the snow, or like a healing hug. She had explained why his life had been the way it was and there was actually hope in the knowledge she had imparted to him. Yet later, after the new year, she told him she was being forced to change her CPN work to a different part of Aberdeen and had no choice but to drop all her patients in Culter. That day he was sad and there was no healing hug, no future and he was angry at the government for all the cuts which were probably the sole reason the next appointment with her would be the last. He considered buying her some chocolate muffins from the new bakers in Culter, but he didn't and turned up that final day empty handed, determined not to get upset.

Once the hour had passed he shook her hand, though he would have liked to give her a healing hug of his own, and she told him it had been a pleasure being his mental hygienist.

Over the last few appointments she'd persuaded him to start at the Psychotherapy Department. She told him about the Hub Group, involving other people with the same illness and where he would learn about a way of thinking called Mentalisation. He would have to go to the hospital and, despite the free lunch, or the fact that more women suffered from the illness than men, the real reason he said yes to it all was he would be left adrift with no shrink, mini-shrink or mental hygienist. She told him he'd get an appointment once he'd reached the top of the waiting list and that he'd have a few one-to-one sessions with a therapist who would assess him. Ash had read the pamphlet she'd given him over a few times and gone on a website that basically gave the same information.

On their last day she had shook his hand. He had hardly ever looked at her because she was too beautiful. Sometimes he'd take off his glasses and short-sightedly stare, but mainly it hurt to look at her because he was afraid he might cry. On their last day she had shook his hand and told him it had been a pleasure being his CPN and it had been like she had given him a chocolate muffin instead.

'Well,' Ash said, 'you're the first CPN I've got through that I haven't given a story to read.' And she laughed, and as beautiful women do, she was more beautiful when she smiled. Ash took one last look back that last day, and Ash decided to smile.

Chapter Eight

It was a beautiful day, a Sunday, and he woke up at about one in the afternoon. So what if he'd run out of legal highs, he couldn't be bothered with the hassle of going into Town to get more. He put on *Northsound 1* and, as the latest hits played, he remembered that he'd taken the two days of his weekend meds on Saturday. A chill came over him, but he warmed up with a bit of dancing on his red carpet to the songs on the radio. Somehow he felt so happy and he didn't have anything, legal highs or pills, only the ability to dance, the freedom to dance all day if he wanted to. So he head banged to the nearest shop, making up moves as he rushed out into the sunshine. Of course he needed cigarettes. The sun disdainfully dragged him down the sun-stretched slope of the road, into the shop to buy a can or two cokes, but to Ash's dismay, the cans of beer brown fizz had sold out. He felt a sudden shudder as the gates of happiness clanged down and, like a sleepy robot, ignoring its function, he bought instead a couple of cans of Tenants lager.

When he got back there was a text from Veronica. He would look at it later and he had his first can and third cigarette of the day. He picked up the house phone and raced through to the bedroom and slowly lay back on his well-pummelled pillows with his lager, kissing small sips like it was a lover lain on top of him. But with each tender sip angry thoughts overtook him, curses and rants aimed at the theatrical characters in a lifelong play he was never going to finish. Linda had asked him to write these thoughts down and he went back into the sitting room, but instead of picking up his journal and pen, he looked at the text.

Hi Ash just to tell you dad has gone into Aberdeen Royal Infirmary.

Fuck, he went to the house phone. Veronica's message told him.

Hi Dad had a fall this afternoon and he's in the hospital, I'm here too, please call.

Ash stabbed in her number.
'Are you all right?' he asked.
'Are you all right?' he asked again.
'What happened?' He was starting to get annoyed.
'Oh, Ronnie was changing a light bulb in Dad's kitchen and got his foot caught in a rung, lost his balance and landed on Dad.'
Pathetically he said he had had a drink.
Vers angrily said his name like a curse.
'Why've you had a drink?'

'I got them before the messages.'

He started to cry. He heard her husband's voice calling from further away on the phone.

'Pull yourself together.'

'What did that fucking man say?' He shouted back, crushing the tears from his eyes.

'Ash, I can't talk to you when you're like this,' Ver said.

'OK then, just tell me what ward he's in.'

Soon Ash found himself back down the shop buying eight cans of Tennants and as soon as he got back, he quickly went through them, glugging and gulping them down, not like they were his lover but his rapist. He stayed up all night sending off countless text and voice messages to Ver's answerphone. They ranged from,

'Please call me back,' to,

'I'm big and fat enough to squish his fucking mother, how'd he like that?

In the morning, he went to the chemist, red faced, for his daily med with tears in his red, night-swollen eyes. 'My dad's in hospital.' He staggered out onto the street stopping himself from sobbing anymore. He went and got his rations in the Spar as he did every day.

When he got home the full depth of his night's drinking drenched him. He hadn't felt it before as he'd been so angry. Yet he wanted to start calling again, but he didn't have strength, or the desire left to do so. He had to pull himself together and go and see his dad in the hospital. As an afterthought, he told himself, I can get some legal highs when I'm in town.

Still red-eyed and in the same clothes he'd been wearing all night, he grabbed his bag threw in the book he'd been reading by Kazou Ishiguro, *When We Were Orphans* and rushed down to the bus stop. He jumped into the book as soon as he took his seat, reading frantically until he got to the junction onto Union Street. He closed the book and asked the older man beside him if he knew which bus would take him up to ARI. 'I think it's the 13, but I'm not sure.' Ash breathed lager fumes at him.

'That's OK, I'm pretty sure it's the 59.' He proceeded to tell the old guy about his dad being in hospital. 'I don't know what he's going to do, he loves walking his dog down by the River Don. As he was moving to get off the bus, the man said, 'You don't have to get off here, you can get the 59 on Union Terrace.' Ash asked him if he was from Edinburgh. 'No,' he replied.

Ash smiled. 'You sound like you're from Edinburgh, but then everybody sounds like there from Edinburgh these days. Excuse me; I'm getting off here so I can get some cash from the bank.' The guy laughed. Ash thought, he probably thinks I'm going to get drunk again.

Once he'd got some cash from the hole in the wall he dashed down to the market, got his Clockwork Orange, then somehow got on the right bus to the hospital. Eventually he found the ward after nearly breaking down again, angry and exhausted by the confusing long corridors to the lifts. A nurse gave him a concerned look as if he were a patient escaping from his own ward. He found the lift to the ward and got a supply elevator up and up.

'Can I see William?' he asked the nurse he saw as soon as he came in the door.

'Yes, sure you can.'

He was over there on his own, the bed a corpse beneath him. Each ringing step on the linoleum floor of the ward sounded like an angel dying. Ash pulled up a seat near the sleeping head of his old man.

'Hello there.' Dad's head turned his way and it almost seemed to be smiling.

'Oh, I've brought you some cakes.' He put them on the bedside cabinet.

'Help me sit up, will you,' Ash's dad said. Ash went behind the top of the bed and tried to gently lift him. He was afraid he would hurt him as he pushed up on to the pristine pillows. Ash's dad felt as heavy as kryptonite. Dad had almost fallen asleep again. 'I'll get you a cake from the box.' Ash chattered away as he ate. 'Did you like it?'

'It's too sweet, they give me heartburn.'

'Sorry.'

'That's all right.' He began to fall asleep and Ash stayed a little longer. He startled awake and he smiled at Ash as if he had forgotten he was there. Ash told him he was off now.

'Yeah, that's OK, I'll just go back to sleep.'

Ash wanted to get on the bed beside his frail father and go nowhere else, hold him, give him all his own strength and life, grabbing him back from the gates of paradise, but instead he got up from the chair and kissed him on the forehead.

Then he trotted out of the ward, afraid to look back, to his journey back home and his Clockwork Orange.

Chapter 9

Ash slept fitfully that night, but those moments of sleep were dream-doused. When he at last got up with the alarm he remembered that today was to be an eventful day. He was to meet his psychotherapist for the first time. He'd got plenty of time so ironed a shirt, showered and cleaned the mud off his boots. Afterwards, he still had plenty of time, but the late August sunshine manhandled him out the door. Still, as he got on the bus into town, he knew he would be at least two hours early for the appointment and, apart from picking up legal highs, Ash couldn't think of anything much else to do. Yet he was relieved when he had made it into town and got off at Holburn Street to take out some cash from the machine. If he walked slowly down Union Street it'd take maybe fifteen minutes to get to the market, then another ten minutes for a coffee, then a slow walk up to the hospital would kill enough time to maybe get something to eat up there.

But, despite himself, he raced with his normal long strode and swift plod to the market. Instead of fifteen it only took him five minutes to get to the counter in the market and was soon back on the teeming Union Street outside McDonald's, but he wasn't feeling hungry. Ash knew he would later and, he didn't particularly want to eat in the hospital canteen, so he retraced his steps back up Union Street, past Waterstones up to the Co-op, got a jar of coffee, cigarettes and a couple of ready meals. Now, only an hour and a half until he had to be at the Psychotherapy Department.

He crossed over Union Street into the newest cafe in town, which used to be the old Waterstones, and sat by the window with a flat white. He noticed a gay guy watching him and tried not to catch his eye. Halfway through the coffee he went to the toilet and on his way out the gay guy was there. Ash gave him a dirty look even though he was annoyed with himself that the guy had presumed he was a faggot and probably wanted Ash to suck him off in the toilet.

Ash had thought, I wish they would leave me the fuck alone.

Back before his flat white he felt old and dishevelled, he'd shaved rather badly. He stared out the window, looking across at the dentist where he'd recently missed an appointment. As Ash stared he saw a fat Ned. The Ned stared back at him, gave the look and a hateful smirk at his curls of hair and the flowery shirt Rachael had given him for Christmas. He hated queer bashers worse than queers. Draining his cup he got out of the place. There was nothing else for it, he would go up to the hospital and be early, why was he always so fucking early.

He lit up with Helen's lighter and tossed the butt down on Union Terrace. The hospital had a new anti-smoking policy and no one was allowed to smoke in the grounds. So he sparked up another and puffed away up the road past Rosemount Square, throwing it down at a junction across from a hairdresser he used to frequent and a bookshop he used to haunt on giro days.

As he walked the last wee while to the side entrance to the hospital, the Green Door, he was suddenly surprised to see the Green Door was gone. To Ash, it remained the symbol of his countless visits to the hospital and someone had taken it away and he felt a sense of loss and anger. For a bloody door, he thought, come on, pull yourself together. He had an hour or more to wait now he was here and he sauntered around the grounds looking for the Psychotherapy Department. He'd never to been to that part of the hospital before, but he found it relatively quickly. He fiddled with Helen's lighter and found a garden round the back of the building with a bench and hot flowers in the August sun. Despite the prohibition on smoking in hospital grounds, he felt he had no choice but to light up again. There was no one about and, even if there were, he doubted he'd get a section for breaking the rules, at most a few dirty looks from people in offices about the garden. He looked again at his watch. Ages yet. His eyes scanned the light green lawn ahead of him. He saw a magic mushroom. He was tempted to pick it, chew and swallow it down with the can of coke in his bag. He knelt down to get a closer look. His hand almost unconsciously searching out the tiny, wee, pointy pleasure to take it up, but he left it and the used cigarette smouldering in the grass, telling himself it wouldn't be a good idea seeing the psychotherapist for the first time dinging out of his face.

Ash went out of the garden to find somewhere else to sit in the sun, the legal highs burning a hole in his pocket, but a joint was probably out of the question too. When there was only a half hour until his appointment, he ventured into the Psychotherapy Department, found the receptionist, and said he was in for an appointment with Martin Templeton. Ash wondered to himself whether he was a doctor, is that what you call a psychotherapist. It was confusing after seeing a psychiatrist for such a long time. In the waiting area he took out the Alan Warner book he was halfway through, *Morvern Callar*, and read until the time of his appointment. There were a few others waiting, all with their heads down looking at the floor, lost inside themselves. Ash had said hello, but most of them had barely responded. He got stuck into the book. Finally, at two, the portly psychotherapist came through from his office, saw Ash straight away, and came over to him.

'Are you Ash?' Ash responded with a smile and shook the proffered hand. 'Come through.'

Most of the appointment went by in a blur. Martin told him he was here for an assessment and for him to see how Borderline Personality Disorder had affected

159

his life. Martin Templeton told him he had lived in Chester, the same place Ash had lived in his childhood. Deep inside Ash there were still constant storm blasts of anger sure that he was only here because of NHS cuts. He was fine with the psychiatrists and CPNs, that here with Martin he was just going over old ground as he answered the therapist's questions. So basically he felt he was being fobbed off and getting second best. Martin asked about his relationship with his daughter, his sister, Vers, their Father, implying some kind of red necked incest when he asked about his cousin in Australia, yet cut him off when Ash tried to speak about his dead mother. Ash wanted to cry.

Martin talked about Mentalisation, which was an aid for people with Borderline Personality Disorder, to get their emotions under control to help them in situations with others and to take responsibility for their own thoughts.

The psychotherapist, doctor whatever the fuck he was, asked him if he wanted to join a Mentalisation course, called The Hub Group, every Tuesday for six months. Ash felt this was the last chance for him and the anger dissipated. Ash would be able to spend time with others like him, maybe learn what exactly this so-called BDP was and not feel so lost and alone, knowing other people were going through the same thing.

Then the tears came and he started blurting out, thinking, it has been a long time since my last confession. Yet as the words spewed from his dry lips,

Ash felt he was explaining what he was sure had caused his illness, not child abuse, or drugs, not being moved around from pillar to post with Dad in the Navy, but this, these words of those days broken and lost when he had run away to London.

'I'd got a job in a gay bar, hated it and I put on a bit of a gay act, but I met an Aussie guy there who offered me a job in his start-up business and a place to stay after I'd got the sack for stealing from a charity box. I stayed with him a long time,' Ash laughed. 'But I managed to save my arse. We ended up staying in a posh place just off Regent Street and I worked quite hard helping with his business, which was taking off. But then he started drinking a lot and I had to get away from him, stealing £200 on the way out the door. I went to Soho to get a prostitute. Her name was Teen. I had a bit of an adventure with her, hitch-hiking up to Fife where she abandoned me, all £200 gone. Instead of going back home to Aberdeen, Teen had told me there was a club in Soho that'd love to have me so I borrowed money from my Grandmother and got on the next bus back to London. I became a stripper in a place called Colts. The first night there I was dancing downstairs and some gang who wanted to close Colts down invaded the place and all the punters scrambled for it. I was left alone and one of the gang came up to me and grabbed my dick. I was terrified and he told me to get the fuck back to Glasgow or wherever I was from. He squeezed my cock really hard and I thought he was going to cut it off.

Suddenly about a hundred cops came out of nowhere and the guy scarpered.

'Anyway, once it all calmed down, one of the other strippers gave me a line of speed — that was first time I took speed. I chewed on my teeth all night, see that's why my teeth are all pushed in and squinty like that. So, in the end, I stayed at Colts, stripping along to Kate Bush songs, sleeping in an armchair by the poppers, where the punters paid the cash to get in. Oh it seemed that way forever and all I did with the money was buy drink. I hardly ate, I even tried to get help from the Aussie guy, but he had a new flatmate and had told him I had AIDS. In the end, after being in an endless David Lean epic, I ran away from London back home.'

Ash came to a breathless stop, yet the words kept rattling through his head. There had been so much more, he'd made a few friends, stayed in a homeless hostel, gone to Cornwall, ate a Wimpey quarter pounder each night he stayed in a B&B in Victoria. But now he could only cry, he joked though through his tears.

'Somehow I managed to save my arse throughout it all'

Mark Templeton listened through it all; maybe he had expected something different. What? That his father beat him, or his mum stuck Kirby grips in his penis at bath times? Ash presumed he'd heard it all from other people, all their cries for help, all their confessions, it was his job after all, he probably thinks I'm some kind of tinky smackhead. Isn't that enough, Ash screamed in his head, wouldn't all of that have fucked up anyone?

Then, before Ash knew it, the hour and the appointment was over. The tears had stopped by then. Psychotherapist Templeton filled out an appointment card for the next time and, as he left, Ash said to himself, All I wanted was to speak about my mum, how she's gone and I'm still here and it's wrong.

But he said, 'See ya next week.'

Chapter Ten

Ash was going to see his new girlfriend. They'd had long walks together down by the River Don — a long stretch of moss green-white, and sky reflecting on the blue-black water. Ash would take pictures of her there in her white and black coat.

Her name was Maxi, and she was William's dog. Ash had once called her Mad Max 2, back in the days when she'd run away from him, barking hysterically, or cowering away from him in the safety of William's bedroom every time Ash visit. Now, since Dad's last fall and stint in hospital, a great sea of change had occurred. She'd bark happily and cadge pieces of chicken from the tins of Big Soup Chicken and Veg that William made for lunch. One day Maxi had even climbed on his lap, and pawed his face, as if she was his best pal in the world, and he was keen to take the dog around the large field outside the house.

Since William's last fall he hadn't been able to take her out much. How the old man had loved to take her along the river or along the railway line, but now all he could manage was the quick drive to ASDA for coffee in the cafe, a little bag of shopping. So instead, Ash or his sister would take Maxi. Maxi was a good dog and liked getting her picture taken.

Maxi was waiting at the gate for Ash as he went up the steps and into William's bit. He was in the kitchen putting on his jacket.

'Just caught me on the way out.'

Maxi followed Ash through to the downstairs toilet, two buses worth of repressed urine spilled from him. 'Are you going up to ASDA?'

'Where else.'

He took Maxi to the car and put her on the dog-hair-covered pink sheet on the backseat and gave her a sausage. She took the treat and gulped it down; while William was slowly making his way from the house he gave her another. When they were both in the car, William asked him if he'd walk to the health centre later and pick up a prescription and put it in the chemist.

In no time, William raced to the parking lot, getting a slot straight away in the disabled parking space nearest the front of the shopping centre.

'Tie up the dog.' Ash got out smashing the door into a 4x4 parked illegally.

Inside, William went straight for the cigarette counter.

'Is it still muddy by the river?' Ash asked, as he hadn't been to the river all winter with Maxi.

'It was yesterday when Alexa took her.'

'Oh.' Ash had suddenly run out of things to talk about now they were sitting in the cafe. He was hungry, but the entirety of Dyce School all seemed to be in the queue getting their second breakfast. Ash surveyed them, hoping there'd be some food left once they'd had their fill.

He poured sugar sachets into his coffee and stirred it roughly with the complimentary brown stick. 'I think I'll get a roll and sausage.'

'Go on then, they aren't as bad as they look.'

'I'll wait.'

'Coward.'

'Lisa was giving me a hard time about all the sugar I take.'

'Just ignore her.'

'But I do need to cut down.'

'Don't worry about it. I imagine Rachael'll have to look after you when you can't shit properly and clean you up.'

Ash stared at him.

'I doubt it. She barely speaks to me anymore.'

His father wasn't listening; he'd seen Alexa, his neighbour, and de facto dog walker, when Ash or his sister wasn't about.

'Hi,' Ash said as she came over and sat beside them. She was a widower and had been actively wooing William before William broke his hip. Since then he hadn't gotten as angry at her for 'popping in' or giving him 'indigestible food'. In fact, recently he'd called her a' god send' and 'irreplaceable'. Ash recalled his teenage years trying to read books in his bedroom or trying to study and her two sons were endlessly revving their motorbikes just outside the house in the car park. Now, the last time he'd seen the eldest of the two brothers he'd looked a well-heeled, respectable business man, whereas Ash, in comparison, looked like a dishevelled dosser in comparison.

Ash never knew what to say to them so he usually stuck to safe subjects such as Donald Trump, decimalisation and the different drugs he was on, all of which would get William talking. Yet Ash had been trying to make a special effort not to wind up his father, intentionally or unintentionally, since the tumult of his recent drug and drinking incidents and especially since his last fall. On the main he succeeded and his visits, usually unannounced and sometimes following the same routine, both well-oiled and mutually sustainable. Ash veered off Obama, the EU referendum, and the Plight of the Palestinians and tried his best to keep to a censored version of his life. He would tell him of the ups and downs of The Hub, or Mentalisation Group and avoided talking too much of the fall in oil prices as this would lead to pangs of guilt, i.e. Lisa's mum perhaps losing her job at Shell and his almost daily guilt trip of not having a job and being an inadequate father.

Thankfully, by the time Alexa got her coffee from the contrary coffee machine, the queue at the till had quickly diminished and Ash rushed to get his roll and sausage. The woman at the till was another Alexa. She didn't smile much, but she was friendly enough.

William had told him she'd gone out for a fag during her break and thrown down the filter and a keen-eyed refuse inspector fined her £40 on the spot. Ash had looked about the car park of the shopping centre from the car at the time and quipped, 'If they fined everyone £40 every time they threw down a butt the fucking deficit would have gone by now.'

He got two sachets of tomato sauce as he smiled and paid Alexa with his debit card and went back to the table with his roll and sausage where William and Alexa were talking. He lathered the sausages with the sauce, licking away the last few spots on the side of the sachets.

'You sure you've got enough sauce on there?' He always asked that and Ash felt like a wee boy with his Sunday morning fry up, dumping artistically half a bottle of HP sauce on the rashers of bacon, sausages, tomatoes, fried bread and mushrooms.

'You won't be able to taste the bloody sausage.' William's voice broke him from gastronomic reverie.

'That's the point.' He tried to laugh but his mouth was full of roll and sausage. When he had finished and Alexa had gone Ash asked, 'What do you need from the store? I can go round and pick it up for you.'

'No. No, it's the only exercise I get and if I don't people will wonder what has happened to me.'

'I'd probably get it wrong anyway.' Ash recalled the dog food incident and the soup incident when he'd got a six pack of jelly, not gravy, and mulligatawny soup instead of lentil.

'Yes, but you can carry some of the big stuff.'

Once William had divested himself of the cafe chair and table, Ash surged ahead to glance at the DVDs in the window of the Media Centre then got a basket. Ash got the plastic bag at the self-service tills which William used to carry about the shop. He met him at the plants display.

'What big stuff do you need?'

'Oh, don't rush me.'

'OK, sorry.'

Ash hovered about his dad for a while, then popped round the aisle to look at the meagre display of books near the stationery and then got a red diary and a packet of twenty pens, then went searching for Dad. He was still at the flowers,

'You remember the tulip bulbs you bought me?' Ash asked.

'Yes.'

'Well, I went out into the garden to plant them, and Vers, in one of her epic clear-outs of my house, had thrown away my trowels.'

'She does that all the time to me. I couldn't find any of my bookmarks the other day. Which reminds me will you get some from the library?'

For a moment Ash thought he had made a joke, but William was convinced knowing her who had a penchant for throwing out good stuff with the bad. Ash didn't want to remember the extensive lighter collection removal incident, as it just made him angry. Of course, later in the year, he had to clear out his loft and discovered the three trowels and felt a sense of guilt for always blaming his good sister Vers for everything that went wrong. At least at the start of the week he had improvised by digging holes for the bulbs with his bare hands. And he was looking forward to spring when they came to flower.

'Could you get me a big box of Corn Flakes — not the biggest but the one down? And some dog biscuits?'

'Sure.' Ash sped off from the sell-by date collection of the very chilly aisle. William usually spent a long time there but never bought a thing, however, by the time Ash had found the cereal and Maxi's biscuits he was nowhere to be seen. Ash walked hurriedly up and down the aisles and along the central one, peering up and down. He was beginning to get anxious. He eventually found him looking at the kitchen bins near the clothes section.

'Oh there you are. I thought you had your invisibility ring on.'

'I don't have one of them,' William said tiredly, as if instead of his son, he had been rushing about the aisles.

'I was only joking.'

'I know. Can you carry this bin for me?'

'OK.'

Then a voice behind him said, 'Is that you Ash?'

And he turned and there was Faith, he was pretty sure it was Faith. His head asked, 'Is that you Faith?'

He thought he had sat beside her one day on the bus going in for legal highs, but he had mistaken her for someone who, now he thought about it, must've been Charlotte, flashing her wedding ring at him. On the bus he'd been thinking, Who is this? For months he had been convinced it'd been Faith and the more he told the story to the more certain he was it had been Faith that day, on the bus, but it hadn't been Faith at all. The woman with the trolley with a child in the seat was definitely a great love of his life. He'd dumped Faith when Lisa's mum got pregnant and for the first few drunken years after Lisa had been born, the woman he had searched for whenever he was in town, whom he'd call when he'd drunk too much and cried like a bairn. Her. Here. In front of him like a heart attack.

'Hi,' he said, smiling. At least he hoped he was smiling. He'd only dreamt about her once and he had found out she was married when he looked her up on Facebook. 'Who is this?'

'This is Rian.' she said.

'Are you helping your mum get shopping?' Come on Ash, he told himself, you haven't seen her for sixteen years, you could think of something better to say than that. Faith was a blonde now, not a bottle redhead, and not much like the photos he kept of her in a blue covered album Mum had given him. She's older now but she still looked young, but then she had been younger than him when they'd gone out. 'So are you going to help your mum to get sweeties?' Rian looked at him, but didn't smile.

'No. No sweeties for you,' her mum said.

They must've spoken more; Ash wondered later. Oh yes, he remembered, she asked him why he was in Dyce and he said he'd come to see his dad.

Faith smiled as Ash looked at his father quietly looking at clocks nearby. 'Is he still with us?'

And yes, he recalled, he had gone on about his cats, one of which was almost twenty-one and had been around all those empty years ago when Faith would tell him to give the cat more attention. But, the conversation didn't last long, not long enough. It could never have been long enough. Here, in ASDA, where he never saw anyone he knew. He turned back to his dad once he'd said goodbye. He could have talked, prattled on, but he didn't want to prattle on, so he turned away and for the rest of the shopping experience he felt he was drunk and stoned and he'd been hit on the head.

Then again, just before they made it to the Satan-inspired self-service checkouts, he saw Faith again when he got some cheap tuna for the cats and she was getting a tin of shrimps. Faith asked, 'So how old is your daughter now?'

'Fifteen, sixteen this year.'

'Has it been that long? Do you still see her?'

'Oh yes.' He thought, I'm sorry. I'm sorry. I'm sorry. He said, 'It was good to see you.'

'Yes. You too.' In the field outside the shopping centre as he walked Maxi back from Boots and the library, all his recent dreams and nightmare sped unremembered through his head, sixteen years of déjà vu flooding through him almost like magic mushrooms dancing. He gripped hard on the leash and the bag with his father's Tamazepan thinking, You can't do anything about it. She's married now. She's not mine any more.

Chapter Eleven

Just before Christmas the era of Ash's use of legal highs came to an abrupt and unexpected end.

He was seeing Lisa later in the afternoon, but he had no smoke, so he went into town six hours early. He'd started going to the head shop on King Street which was cheaper than the one in the market. It had only been open a month or two yet already someone, probably the local council, had staved in the window. This lot were usually out of it on their wares and a few times he had blagged a gram or two as the guy serving him seemed to have had lost his ability to count. However, on this particularly frosty Christmas shopping horde filled day, the woman, a blonde, sensibly dressed, clear of eye, who was obviously one of the owners, was on the counter.

'Can I have three grams of Clockwork Orange?'

'We haven't any,' she said, bluntly.

'Where's the list with the other brands on?'

'There's no list.'

'Oh.' The penny dropped. 'So is that the end of it. Are they banned again?'

'For now.' Crestfallen and confused he walked, shoulders straight, out of the door onto King Street, a street with more hairdressers and barbers on it than the For Sale or For Lease signs in the rest of Aberdeen. Now he had what felt like half a century until he saw his daughter so with a wallet full of cash, fresh from the hole in the wall on Union Terrace, he crossed over the dual carriageway, past the Arts Centre to the nearest barbers. A sexy barber, blonde in the prerequisite tight jeans, quickly de-mopped his grey mass of hair. He made a stuttering, nervous conversation about the shootings in Paris

'I was thinking it could've been the Cafe Central on Belmont Street and kids at a bloody concert like the Music Hall. It is all going too far.'

'I know,' she said, sadness in her reflected eyes as she brushed up the grey curls of his hair.

As he sat there, Ash tried to think what to do, and as soon as the tip left his pocket, he sped to the market. Even though he knew it would be the case, both the fancy head shop, which he never used, or the stall further on that he used doggedly, had no Clockwork Orange or legal smokes, snorts, or pills. He went up the side stairs, past the shoplifter's door of British Home Stores, onto Union Street and by the time he was at McDonalds, he had an irritating itch at the back his head. He envisioned that his only options were that a year from now he'd either be a smack head, a crack addict or worse, he had given up drugs completely. He went into McDonalds and ordered two hamburgers and a carton of milk. Or, he thought as he sat down his stomach churning with hunger and fear, I'll be drinking again. Ash had been so proud of himself that he'd not had a drink for over a year and was keen on reminding the folk at the Hub Group every Tuesday.

His head was going, Damn. Damn. Damn, I'll lose it or get beaten up or arrested. Again. Even a half bitter will probably get me stabbed down a dark alley down the wharf as the harbour was now being touted as.

Of course! He had no other choice, he had to call Alison. He'd seen her once since he'd taken the legal stuff and that was because he stupidly bought a particular brand of legal high that was so strong he quickly began to go loopy after the second drag of the first joint.

Her phone, may all the angels of paradise be praised, was answered and he heard Alison's timid voice speaking like triumphant hope.

'I'm seeing Lisa later,' he told her after she said she'd get him something. 'But we might be going to see *Star Wars*, so I might not be able to get there 'til later.' Alison said that was fine. Ash was almost crying with relief. As he left McDonalds a security guard began walking towards him with a suspicious look in her eyes as if she knew he was making a deal on the phone, but he made it to the cold, dirty street feeling now as light of spirit as he was of hair.

His goal now was to see Lisa buy her some shoes and get out of town to Alison's ASAP. Fuck *Star Wars*. The DVD will probably be out in January. Even so, it was going to be a long day, but the light at the end of the tunnel was suddenly so bright. As quickly as he could, he got out of Christmas Shopping Central and snuck down Belmont Street, a colder yet much quieter region, thinking he could sit in the library for a while. At the hole in the wall at the top of Belmont Street, opposite the art gallery, a beggar sat forlorn in the wind, so, hoping the guy would bring him luck, Ash gave him a quid and told the boy to take care of himself, and was wished a Happy Christmas.

Ash wandered down to Union Terrace Gardens, which, after all the fuss a few years ago, had not been revamped and would undoubtedly be never be revamped. The place was deserted, not even an alcoholic urinating in one of the alcoves just below street level. Up on the terrace there was a Street Market and a spinny. A sickening-looking funfair ride, alongside an ice-skating rink which was put up for the holy festivities. He went back up the steps again and crossed over to the library. The wind was sharp and gritty on Rosemount Viaduct. Walking against the wind was his old drinking buddy with a scarf about his face, grey haired, balder and looking older than he usually did.

'Hi, Steve.'

Ash thought that he was going to walk right past him, blank him, but now that he had become a Jehovah's Witness such rudeness was probably a sin. Steve was with his mother.

'We're going to the theatre cafe,' Steve told him.

'I'm just popping into the library. I might join you later,' Ash lied.

The cold and the wind at his back moved him on up the steps of the library and he soon was in the thankful warmth of the fiction department. He went straight to 'I' and picked out a copy of *A Pale View of the Hills* by his recent friend and inspiration Kazou Ishiguro. Typically, there was a copy of the man's latest novel *The Buried Giant*. He told the young, male librarian at the desk 'I ordered *The Buried Giant* from my brother-in-law for Christmas as I'd lost the copy I got for my fiftieth birthday. And there it was all the time.'

'Typical,' the boy at the desk agreed with.

Just over four hours until I see Lisa, Ash thought as he loitered at a free trade stall near the library entrance where coffees, teas and some charity goods were on display, like a fine chessboard that immediately caught his eye.

'I'll get this coffee; I'm exhausted after all the wandering around the library. You know I completely forgot where 'I' was in the alphabet.' This garnered a laugh from the old woman serving. 'Well, Happy Christmas. I'd get the chess board but I've no one to play chess with. I tried to teach my daughter. Not interested. Happy Christmas,' Ash repeated putting the overpriced, morally sound instant coffee into his bag beside the precious, beautiful library book.

Then back out into the cold. He wasn't quite sure what to do next so he watched the ice skaters on the rink in the Christmas Market and tried not to throw up the hamburger while he watched the spinny funfair ride that he dearly hoped Lisa didn't want to go on. Nearby he went into a couple of charity shops and the comic shop, buying a blue T-shirt with *Hope* written on it — he had another at home but the word had faded away. Finally, he went in The Shack and got a flat white from the waitress whom he'd heard was writing a book. He lingered in the coffee shop for a while. He wanted to go up to Alison's, it wasn't far away, but he didn't want to be wasted when he saw Lisa.

I suppose I should buy some Christmas presents for other people, Ash concluded. He forged his way to Waterstones. As he sped down to Union Street, he saw a painted wooden cat in one of the market stalls. Alison'd like that, he thought, but he kept on going and didn't get it. By the time he got to the bookshop and traipsed around a few times, feeling like a shoplifter, he felt tired and called his sister on his mobile. No answer, so he sent a text upstairs, while having another coffee, which she quickly replied writing that she was in the hallowed Union Square.

Despite the fact that he was trying to waste time until he saw Lisa he almost ran through the overpriced, hot arena of consumerism and, breathless and sweating, he plonked himself down across from where Vers was sitting. She smiled at him as she was eating one of the

Starbucks chocolate mallow-on-a-stick specialities. As Ash tried to get his breath back, she asked, 'Have you bought any presents yet?

Earlier in the week he'd arranged to meet Vers for their annual present buying ritual, but that day he had enough Clockwork Orange and a persistent sniffle so he cancelled it.

'No. Not really. I'm going to buy Lisa some shoes today so she can pick them out herself. I'm sure I've got wrapping paper at home, but if you want to wrap it up yourself feel free as you 'threw out' my sellotape you can have this jar of coffee.'

Vers laughed scornfully. 'I told you what I wanted. Do you want me to write it down for you?'

'Yes.'

He looked down the list. 'A massage voucher?'

'Yes, for a place on Crown Street across from the old post office.'

'Oh. OK. My back is killing me. If I lie on the table would you give my back a good kneading? You said you wanted a diary. I got myself a page-a-day one. I'm going to write a novel called *The Sun Doesn't Shine Like That Anymore.*'

'What's it about?'

'The last few years or so.'

'Well, when it's finished, I'll get all my friends at church to read it.'

'I don't think they'd like it very much.'

'They have good ones in John Menzies.'

'Good what?'

'Diaries. I need one with a week on two pages.'

'OK. I'm going to try and get a coffee.'

'Get me one of those mango fruit salad bowls while you're there.'

Ash looked at the tremendously long queue. 'I might be a week or two. If Armageddon kicks off while I'm away I'll see you in the next life.'

'Ash,' Vers exclaimed in mock anger.

A few Earth hours later, Lisa and Ash, were in the back row of the cinema, waiting for the film to begin.

What seemed like several days of pure bliss later, when Ash's faith in the scam that was Hollywood was renewed, Ash and his daughter were waiting in the freezing street by the bus stop for her bus home.

Ash said excitedly,

'Do you want to see it again?'

'No,' she said, laughing.

Ash puffed away on a Superking, ignoring the dirty looks from others waiting for a bus. 'Do you have enough change?'

'Yes.'

'You know, being with you, is better than any antidepressant. You're my cure, you know that.'

Lisa gave him a look that was equally one of mirth and pride and surprise, and Ash knew she loved him.

Chapter Twelve

When Lisa went away on the bus, Ash walked quickly up Market Street, thinking again, end of an era. He saw the bus to Alison's at the graveyard. It could pull away at any time now, so he raced ahead to the next bus stop on Broad Street, people-dodging artlessly, panting, his legs over-dosing on lactic acid, panic-filled eyes peering back to see where the bus was. It was slowly gaining on him. He mustered up a sprint of speed as the bus caught up with him at the corner onto Broad Street. Ash sprinted now ignoring the pain in his chest and legs, as he saw the bus had made it to the stop and people had started to get on. He kept going doggedly, as if he had to make the last train to Stockholm to pick up his Nobel Prize for Literature. Just as an old guy on crutches was about to get on, Ash darted past him into the light of the bus and showed his concession card first.

The bus was chock-a-block, but he managed to get a double seat to himself where he proceeded to cough and wheeze, his chest heaving and gasping as he tried to get his breathing under control. By the time he got off the bus, despite getting a few pointed sniggers from a couple of kids, he was feeling cool and controlled, a superhuman in his long black coat.

He knocked on Alison's door and then, after waiting what seemed like ages, knocked again. Eventually, his stomach churning like the spinny sickening funfair thing on Union Terrace, she opened the door. She smiled. 'I was in the bath.'

The long, the short and the tall of it, Ash scored. Though it took a while, he never stopped blabbering out his verbal vomit; there were some heart-stopping moments, changes of plan and waiting. But he scored and the boy even gave him a lift home.

Of course, it was all quiet when he got home. Christmas Eve was a couple of days off, but as he smoked and drank coffee into the dark morning, he remembered that the chemist in the village was closed for four days over the holiday and instead of his daily dispense of pills, he'd get four days' worth of pills. Ash was suddenly dreading it, because, despite his new Hope T-shirt he knew there was no way in hell he'd get through the birthday of God without taking an overdose. And of course, Ash did.

When he'd smoked all the pot, he called Alison.

'You've phoned during Eastenders.'

Oh shit, Ash thought, what have I done.

'And you never left me enough. I had nothing over Christmas.'

'Shit,' he said, apologising several times.

'And the boy wouldn't leave me in peace after he came back from yours.'

'Crap, I'm sorry.'

'Yeah. Me too. Look, I'm watching Eastenders, I'll call you back later.'

'No, it's OK, I'll manage. I'll call in a day or so.'

But when he did, she didn't pick up.

Chapter Thirteen

The day after David Bowie died was a Tuesday so Ash was at the hospital for the Hub Group.

Somehow, he had not bought any drugs, or legal highs, or drank. Mainly because he could not get any, but such is life, and like he'd said to the group, I'm still breathing, I'm still functioning, still on the daily dispense and still going to the Hub Group every week. He'd been walking about Culter, down to the river, or over Ardbeck Moor, taking a memory card full of photos. He'd got back into the new novel he'd started a couple of years earlier and had even applied for a job at the Oxfam Bookshop in town. In fact, to his own surprise, he'd actually painted some of his house and had finished some drawings and paintings that he'd started four years earlier.

For the last two weeks, Martin the psychotherapist had joined the group and they'd been doing some psychodrama. The first day of this, Ash had quickly exited the Group alone while the redhead, tall and freckly pale, with long legs like silk at the touch of his eyes, and an older woman from Seaton. He was pretty sure he was madly in love/lust with the redhead, and the woman from Seaton was like his mother. But, over the next couple of weeks, love/lust turned to hate/lust and, despite the long redness of her hair, freckles that he would play dot-to-dot with, and those legs. She, he concluded, was not bonnier than his daughter.

This Tuesday, the day after David Bowie died, Martin asked them to think of a photograph that they were to use in the psychodrama. Even when Martin asked if Ash had picked a photo, and he'd replied that he was still flicking through them, he knew at once which one he was going to use. Lisa aged six and him with their hobbit feet on Catterline Beach, with Jasper, Vers' old dog. When Martin asked for volunteers to re-enact the picture using other members of the group, Ash said he'd go for it and took centre stage.

'Now,' Martin said, 'tell us about what the picture looks like and choose the group members to be the other people in the picture.'

'OK, well it's me and Lisa and Jasper the dog and we're on Catterline Beach as it's my fortieth birthday, we're standing in triangular tableaux and there's lots of food out of shot that Veronica had made.'

'Pick someone to be Lisa.'

Ash wasn't going to pick the redhead as that would smack too much of favouritism.

'And Jasper.'

One of the other women in the group said she wanted to be Jasper and he picked the other love/lust member of the group, a quiet, almost mute blonde who, all in all, was probably a bit bonnier than his daughter, but only slightly.

'Where do you want them to stand?'

'Like I said, we're in a triangle shape. Lisa's in a rock pool with bare feet, and Jasper's in front looking at the food — chicken and salad cream sandwiches and pizza my sister made.

'She took the photo?'

'Yes.'

'So for a moment,' Martin said, 'tell us how you feel in the photograph.'

'Well I'm happy as it's my fortieth birthday, and I made the choice to go to Catterline.'

'Why did you want to go to Catterline?'

'Well I went out with lassie in Glasgow called Cat before I ended up in Kingseat Hospital. My dad and mum took me there around the same time. I asked him, just to piss him...'

'So, how are you feeling now?'

'Well' I'm happy and I've got no shoes on in it, when I look at the photo, I always call it the hobbit feet pic. Her little ones. My big ones.'

'Why are you happy?'

'It's such a sunny day in July and I feel so free, my hair's longer and darker, and she's happy too, even the dog seems to be smiling.'

'OK, that's good. Now I want you to move Lisa from her position and you stand there and be Lisa.'

'Hello,' Ash said, trying to sound six and rubbed Jasper's head. The woman playing the dog was neither a love/lust or hate/lust object, he wasn't sure what she was. Jasper barked at the undesignated plate of sandwiches.

'So are you having a good day?'

'Yes, it's great!'

'Why?'

'It's so hot and there's so much food. I know there will be some cake and I want to dance in the water.'

'Why?'

'Well I'm having an extra day seeing Daddy as it's his birthday.'

'How old are you?'

'I'm six. There was a deer on the road on the way here.'

'A deer?'

'Yes it jumped right in front of the car, we almost hit it, and that would've spoilt Daddy's birthday if Auntie Veronica had hit it.'

'Did she hit it?'

'No.'

'That's fine then.'

'So, do you like Auntie Veronica?'

'Yes, I think so, she has lots of great cuddly toys and a cool bedroom with a massive wall mirror, but Daddy only shouts when she's with us.'

'Did he shout today?'

'No.'

'Is he enjoying himself?'

'I think he wants to dance about in the water too.'

Ash must've done something, made some facial expression, something changed, that Martin noticed because he suddenly asked in a different voice, as if he wasn't talking to Lisa, but the gnawed soul inside Ash. 'Has something happened?'

And Ash remembered. He didn't want to talk about it, and thankfully Martin quickly moved on.

'Now, Ash, I want someone to be you. Move out of the picture and put someone in your place.'

'OK.' He picked the beardy guy.

'Now you're out of the picture and I want you to speak to the Ash there.'

'What?'

'Just speak to him.'

'OK.'

'Yes,' Martin urged.

Ash said, easily forgetting that moment of awful remembrance, 'Well, I don't know, I'm sorry. Well, you managed to make it to fifty, you might have fucked up so many things, quit things and sometimes given up, but you're still alive and you don't always fuck up, sometimes stick at things and keep going and you don't run away back to London, you keep going and you still keep trying. Er, I'm sorry...'

'That's OK, don't apologise. Now swap places, go back into the picture and the beardy guy can come out again. Talk to him from the picture as if you were talking to you now,'

'This is confusing.' Ash said. (There was something he'd forgotten.)

He went back into the triangle on the hot, hot day in July and spoke to the beardy guy being his fifty-year-old self.

'Hey man what have you done to your hair? You should just chill, you look like you really could do with a drink. Hey don't be so sad, you should be here.'

The beardy guy smiled.

Jasper barked.

'Everything is so beautiful in the heat, man the sun doesn't shine like that anymore.'

Ash heard a voice in his head. He didn't know whose voice it was, it could've been Martin, or the redhead, or Lisa, or Vers, or William, even Dr Straven or all of them. But it does. They told me the sun does shine like that still.

And Ash knew, for once he knew, that it did. And does still.

Chapter Fourteen

Just a day or so after the Brexit Referendum, Ash got drunk with a Bank Holiday weekend's worth of pills in his system. On the whole he managed to not remember much of the night's drinking, and absentmindedly, upon awakening, he wondered who had been in his house with him. His wallet was gone, as well as a large quantity of small change that had filled the old coffee jars scattered just as absentmindedly about the house.

Quickly he cancelled his card with the bank, and then he delightedly discovered that he hadn't lost all his change. Hah! Probably couldn't carry it all. He started to count. Typically, the bank was closed until Tuesday, so he'd have to make do. He bagged-up and set the bags brazenly on the coffee table. They can come back and try to take this, he thought angrily, and then the hangover and the paranoia shocked Ash like a rollercoaster ride.

Why did he have to have gone out? Why?

Apart from Brexit things had been going well, well sort of. Ash had got a part in a play in the local theatre group and yet despite his best efforts, could not remember the meagre lines, unerringly getting them hopelessly mangled at the rehearsals, compounded by the so called clusterfuck he made of moving around parts of the set during an important scene.

Apart from that he got on well with one of the actresses who played the character of his wife. They were the only smokers in the cast, both being sniffed at by Public Enemy No 1. Of course, Ash fell in love with the girl who played a ghost; she had such a beautiful voice when she spoke in character. Ash surprised himself by going with them all to a pub down the road, being sociable and not having a pint, or six. Afterwards, sober at home, he was hyper and worked on a big picture he had started. It was pinned up on the bedroom wall, on a large sheet of paper that took up most of the wall. Later, as the sun was rising, he worked on his book. It was almost finished.

Then one Saturday morning, at an impromptu rehearsal, the play was cancelled. It was the village's gala day and, unshaven and unshowered, he tried to keep ahead of the parade of vintage cars and local groups' floats. When they overtook him Ash saw in the lead car the retired doctor that he had seen a couple of times at the health centre when he first moved here. Ash waved a smile at the group in the car and sped on ahead of the ambling cars and floats, yet only a step or two ahead as if he raced happiness and play. He skipped the corner and went diagonally across The Ploughman's car park. He got a smirk/hate look from a couple of drunken guys, so he sped on, a little wound up, and caught up with the parade that slowly slithered up turning towards the playing field where the gala was being held and Ash was soon once again at the head of the parade. As the cars turned again onto the gala field, Ash carried on up the hill to home, to daily dispense, and a trickster of an idea hidden somewhere about, that he could spend more time searching now he didn't have to read the boring play again.

By Christmas, Donald was President Elect.

The man was inaugurated in front of an unsettled bemused, global-wide audience, some of whom may well have hoped, like Ash, the Final Trump might giggle nervously at the last moment, and say, 'Really, ladies and gentlemen, it was only a joke. Let the lady have it.' Please, we wished.

Ash saw his father over Christmas and New Year and kept his head though all around people were losing theirs. Lately, he'd been going to see him every week and took him around the ASDA in his wheelchair, and of course walked Maxi across the field in front of the house, throwing her discarded plastic bottles to chase and mangle boisterously.

Lisa was sixteen. What the hell had he done for the first sixteen years of the new millennium? But mostly the massacred brain cells had no answer for him. Despite the new cigarette packaging, photos of death and dying, babies' dummies with cigarettes attached, other stark metaphorical images staring up from the ash dusted coffee table, with more warnings than the border between North and South Korea, Ash still chain-smoked.

In the end he finished the big picture, before he finished his book. By Easter he had taken down the picture and pinned up another large sheet of paper. But before he began to draw, he cast down his pencils, his mind in the unwinnable conflict of writing and pictures and tried, for night after night, to write a poem.

Chapter Fifteen

It was the final Thursday of the month, and Ash found himself, as if led by a friendly hand, going to the poetry group on Belmont Street, over the wet cobbles slick with light from the bars and streetlights. Slains Castle Pub looked like a sooty black derelict. Ahead, he saw the art gallery which had been, closed now for two years of renovation. Ash hoped that the galley would reopen soon. He missed going there, it had been always been a thing he did when he was skint. Ash would wander around the various galleries of different forms of art, then go to the library and check out too many books. Afterwards, he would sit on the green benches in Union Terrace garden, have a slow burning cigarette if he hadn't spent all his ciggie rations on booze.

Anyway, Ash turned up the short steps through the yellow doorway of Books and Beans, the walls papered with posters up the flight of stairs into the main part of the book shop, and which had resigned itself to being a coffee shop complete with Wi-Fi, dusty with the books, some never sold since the first day Ash went there to sell some books, and sadly probably never would. Like permanent collage coloured walls.

Recently, when he had come here for a coffee he'd sit and read *Wuthering Heights*, crossly grabbing it from the shelf, bemoaning the almost total inaccessibility to the bookshelves. The place was more of a canteen, he'd storm to himself. Ash would find a place by one of the windows and look at the hungry pigeons on the ledge flying down to the cobbles and across the road to the closed door of the pub club place that he was too old to enter.

Just like the last time he had been to the evening poetry group, the assembled poets had come in a large number and he found a seat nearest the door. Before he could put down his bag and take off his black coat the MC started talking about Tibetan poetry, then introduced a translator guy who spoke of the forms of writing Tibetan poets used. Ash had started to stop listening. He had seen her, the Guinevere girl in her thick jacket and boots that she had on the last time he'd seen her on the cliffs overlooking Dunnotar Castle.

Of course, it had been inevitable that they would meet again, here. Ash had heard of the Guinevere girl the times he'd actually gone to writing groups in the city, but what in the beginning had been a golden certainty that were parts of some story. Ash regretted that he hadn't stuck with the writers' groups and had stopped going altogether never meeting her, and that particular story was never written. Almost as if he'd always shunned happiness. Now, as he sat there looking at her dark hair and her shoulders, he saw that he had left it too late. I've changed, she's probably changed. Jesus, I can't even talk to her.

Ash, however, had come prepared and took a surreptitious quick sip of the half bottle of vodka in the pocket of his jacket and waited for the translator to finish talking. As on the last Thursday of the month, he met Helen. Ash and the Guinevere girl each got a chance to read a poem. She read first.

The Morning Has Spoken

Look. I ordered the sun.
Re-ordered this panoramic day,
this tapestry stitched in time
of heart-crashed hills,
while the white mist rises from the river,
like a happy ghost at play.
Diffusing over houses, our homes,
over field and forest,
with heart spread glee
the morning awakens.
Look. I ordered the blue sky
and added more trees
and now with new birds
the morning has spoken.

Then she smiled at him and Ash took his place, started to read.

A Wanderer

He became strange
stood about streets
as the people passed and posed
staring at the lost old man staring into space.
They never saw the starlings dive.

Ash was standing at the edge of the cliff, looking over Dunnotar Castle iced in snow like a birthday cake on a rumpled dark table cloth of sea.

She stood beside him. Rowena had been helping him with the writing he'd started about King Arthur. He'd even started taking horse riding lessons as research. He'd explained the original idea, the initial tributaries in flood of the exiting of ideas and Helen had helped him focus more, getting the whole book down while ideas were still fresh.

He smiled at Rowena; every time he looked at her was like a surprise. However could she be here? He was as happy as he had been on Lisa's tenth birthday. He took his hand from Rowena's and looked down at the wintry sea clashing against the cliffs, where obstinate seagulls swayed in the air. He pulled out a packet of cigarettes and before Ash lit up, he tossed the packet into the air, they seemed to hover ahead of him held up by the wind, cartoon-like, then fell swiftly and soon vanished into the dark sea and were swept away beyond the castle high on its island.

She kissed Ash, his Rowena, and they turned their back on the castle and the sea, with no regret, because they would see it again some summer's day when an old magic rose, here where joy was always unexpected and love the only cure, his hand in Rowena's beneath the roof of the world, in her hand precious to Helen as handful of jewels, in her he felt that touch leading him, leaving the snow and sea cliffs behind for new strangers to stare at. Then leave.